MY PARENTS' DARKROOM
DEVELOPING THE PAST

MY PARENTS' DARKROOM
DEVELOPING THE PAST

Reinhard Tenberg

YOUCAXTON PUBLICATIONS
OXFORD & SHREWSBURY

Copyright © Reinhard Tenberg 2019

The Author asserts the moral right to
be identified as the author of this work.

ISBN 978-1-912419-87-6
Printed and bound in Great Britain.
Published by Reinhard Tenberg 2019
YouCaxton Publications

YCBN: 0101

'*Human memory is a marvellous but fallacious instrument... It is certain that practice (in this case, frequent re-evocation) keeps memories fresh and alive... But it is also true that the memory evoked too often, and expressed in the form of a story, tends to become fixed in a stereotype, in a form tested by experience, crystallized, perfected, adorned, instilling itself in the place of the memory and growing at its expense.*'

Auschwitz survivor Primo Levi,
The Drowned and the Saved, 1988

'*If we want to meet the dead, looking alive, we turn to art.*'

Hilary Mantel, Reith Lecture, 2018

Chapter 1

I always thought I knew who my parents were. No, I'm not adopted – both of my parents are listed on my birth certificate: 'Cäcilia Wilhelmine Berger, and Karl Rudolf Berger, Photographer'. It even states that I was born at home; our GP was there and he assisted with the birth. My older brother, Helmut, thinks he was friendly with Mum. We were the first post-war generation and, as far as I can remember, we had a happy childhood. We were told there had been a war, and that was that. No further questions. Dad died three years ago, in 2001. I did have some questions then. When Mum had to go into a care home, I started to discover who my parents really were.

The first thing I saw when I entered my mother's flat was a large wooden cigar box sitting on the coffee table. I recognised it immediately. A relic from my childhood. I had come over in order to help clear out the flat in Bad Iburg, a sleepy little spa town near Osnabrück in northern Germany. Helmut had arrived a day earlier and stayed the night in her flat. As always, he was wearing jeans and a black shirt – I don't think he has anything else in his wardrobe – and, apart from his ever-more-receding hairline, he looked unchanged and unaffected by Mum's absence.

'This is yours,' he said, shoving the box towards me, which was sealed at the front with brown parcel tape. It was an unusual box: square, around thirty centimetres. He rolled his eyes with a long-suffering sigh.

'It's got your name on it. Looks like Mum's handwriting. I found it in the cellar yesterday, when I started to clear out her things. No hand grenade in it, I hope. Are you staying for a few days?'

'What do you mean? Hmm, no, I'm sorry – just for the weekend. It's difficult to get away in September; we're busy preparing for the new term.'

'But you are going to visit Mum in her new care home, aren't you?'

'Of course, but I have to fly back Sunday night. I'll go and see her tomorrow.'

'There are a few other bits and bobs on the coffee table – records, nick-knacks and a shoebox full of old photos nobody wants. Help yourself. The rest will go in the skip.'

Grassmann Brasil, batch 406, read the black letters on the cigar box. A large label with *Jonas* in joined-up German handwriting was stuck on the lid. Even before I opened it up, the aroma of unlit cigars returned to my senses – a smell like rain-soaked earth … rich, loamy soil. I remembered Grandma carefully taking the cigars out one by one, each individually wrapped in layers of shiny tissue paper, before handing me the empty box to store my toys in.

There I was, in the backroom of my grandma's tobacco shop, a ten-year-old boy with blond, spiky hair, carefully lifting my toy cars up from between the skyscrapers of New York City, built from tens of smaller, upright cigar boxes piled on top of each other. I used to meticulously line up the cars in my box before taking them with me to her flat, where I'd continue playing on her thick Persian rug. On the way home I always asked permission before jumping into the paternoster lift next door. I was fascinated by this old-fashioned contraption, which consisted of a chain of huge open compartments that moved slowly in a loop up and down, without stopping, inside a multi-storey tower block of flats and shops, so when the floor of the compartment was level with the marble floor of the building you stepped in, and vice versa. Mind you, you had to be pretty agile to catch the right moment to jump in and out. I never dared to stay in and go right up to the twelfth floor and round the other side, for fear that the compartments would turn upside down at the top. Grandma used to wait for me on the ground floor, and made sure I was safe jumping out, and …

'Are you going to open that bloody box or not?' Helmut interrupted my childhood memories. He was looking over my shoulder when I broke the seal. But when he had satisfied himself that there were no valuables to share, he lost interest and began sorting out the kitchen.

Someone, probably my mother, had kept this box with treasures dating from my childhood days. There were a few toy cars, a conch shell and two beautiful periwinkle shells, a small photo album, an old ciné film roll and a scrapbook with the odd photo loosely stuck in. The remnants of days gone by, although fairly well-preserved, had the patina of old age. As I touched them for the first time in more than forty years, each object evoked a distinct memory. The first thing that fell out, when I clumsily opened the scrapbook, was a photograph of me holding a hand grenade.

So that's what Helmut's strange comment had been about. He had obviously not forgotten the day when I'd found it in the rubble and had threatened to detonate it. Mind you, I hadn't had a clue how these things worked. Staring at the photograph, it all came back to me with vivid immediacy. Me, probably about eleven or twelve, arguing with my older brother about my 'treasure'. I remember he was always checking up on me – which I hated.

'What are you doing, Jonas?'
'Nothing.'
'Do you wanna play football on the rec?'
'Why would I wanna do that? I've just been outside.'
'What are you doing, then?'
'I'm busy.'
'What have you got there?'
'Nothing.'
'Yes, you have. I saw you hide something under the bed.'
'Nothing to do with you.'
'Go on, let's see. Is it another body part you've dug up?'
'Get lost.'
'Or a whole body this time?'
'Better than that.'
'What, then?'
'None of your business.'
'You think you're special, don't you? Now you've been allowed to travel to Grandma's on
your own.'
'Compared to you, I am. You weren't allowed at my age.'
'Ha, I've been doing war stuff, you know.'
'What? With the Boy Scouts?'
'We don't just mess about. We are doing proper patrols along the river.'
'It's nothing like being at the Front, like Dad was.'
'He wasn't at the Front, anyway. He was back behind the lines. I know.'
'He was at the Front.'

'I bet you don't know half the things I know. You're too young.'

'I do. And I can prove it.'

'Bloody hell! Where did you—?'

'What's the matter? Never seen a hand grenade before?'

'Is it live?'

'Course it is.'

'Where did you get it?'

'Where do you think? No-man's land, in the rubble. I was digging for treasure.'

'No, you didn't.'

'Did.'

'Let's have a look.'

'No. I could blow you up if I wanted. Bang!'

'Don't do that! Some soldiers didn't throw it quick enough – it blew their brains out.'

'Scared, are you? Look, it—'

'Don't do that! What if it goes off? Give it here, Jonas.'

'It's mine. What's this pin and ring for? Shall I pull it?'

'No. Stop messing about. It'll explode. Give it to me – now!'

'OK, but you need to take a photo of me first, so I can prove I found it. What are you going to do with it?'

'If you give it to me, I won't tell anyone.'

'Here you are. Your hand's shaking. I heard what you said about me downstairs …'

'It's not true.'

'Liar. You didn't want another brother.'

'Stupid.'

'Come on. Blow me up, then.'

'What are you talking about? Come on, let's bury it in the garden.'

5

'OK, I'll just get my camera.'
And so we did: took the picture, dug a deep hole and buried it.

I stuck the photo back in as best I could, without showing it to Helmut. My heart was still racing when I sat down at Mum's desk by the window and began thumbing through the scrapbook. In the middle of the spine, someone had stuck in a page with ragged edges, clearly ripped out from another booklet, or a diary. It was ruled with thick blue lines and full of inky writing that spread over the lines in clusters, spilling over the red margins on the right. There was a date at the top: *20 March 1945*. Then I recognised Mum's handwriting – the old-fashioned German handwriting, just like my name on the cigar box.

Ernsthausen, 20 March 1945
Thank God we've reached the West. But there's still no sign of Rudolf. I am sooo desperate. My love, are you still alive? None of the Feldpost has been getting through for the last two months. Where are you? We have an eight-week-old son. I have called him Helmut; he has his father's eyes. I pray to God that you're still alive.

I can't sleep. And I hope that writing down some of the horrific events of the past weeks will help me to unburden my mind. I'm writing by candlelight because of the nightly bombing raids. We are now with my parents in Ernsthausen. I sent you a letter to your last posting in Liegnitz. The Russians were getting perilously close when we fled; we could hear their tanks pounding Kattowitz. We joined a long

6

trek of refugees. No motor vehicles – I think they've all been requisitioned by the Wehrmacht – just handcarts, prams and some horse-drawn hay carts. Mother had managed to 'organise' an old pram for the baby. She's been so helpful. We walked most of the time, hungry and cold. Snow and ice had left the roads treacherous. Occasionally we were allowed to take our turn on the hay cart, sharing with some heavily pregnant women. They'd escaped from East Prussia. I can still see them: huddled shapes, clothes in tatters, rigid with cold and barely able to stand up. Hollow faces that would not speak. They'd been gang raped by Russian soldiers. Did we deserve all this? I never thought it would all end like this. Mother told me that our flat in Köln is no more. Germany is no more, but we are alive – are you?

I know, a fate like many others, but history books don't tell you these stories in the same way and it becomes personal when it's your own family. What they must have gone through. Not knowing whether Dad was alive or not. Fleeing from the Russians with a small baby. Poor Mum. But why was there only the one page? And where was the rest of the diary? None of us even knew that Mother had written a diary during the war. Helmut seemed unmoved when I showed him the page.

'I know. She was always writing diaries, baby books for each child, what we were able to do at what age, lots of boring children's stuff like that, but she never told us about a war diary – and why should she have done?'

For him, everything that happened before we were born was in the past and should be forgotten. Why should we, the first post-war generation, want to remember the shame and guilt that past generations had bequeathed us? Why should we shoulder the blame for what our parents did? He wanted a final *Schlussstrich*, a line drawn under the past, redesignating it as 'history', whereas I forever sought to keep the flame of memory alive. We argued a lot about the importance of commemorating historical events. I remember him visiting me in London for a few days in June and making some derogatory remark about the airtime given to commemorate the sixtieth anniversary of the D-day landings of Allied troops in Normandy. Hundreds of the last surviving D-Day veterans had gathered on both sides of the English Channel; sixty years on from the decisive World War Two mission. Bush, Blair, Chirac, Schröder, and other world leaders joined to commemorate this momentous event.

Living for the here and now was the only thing Helmut cared for – freedom and oblivion. But for me freedom and oblivion make strange bedfellows. How can you find the path to your own future, know yourself, if you don't know where you've come from? The past has shaped us, our parents' past has shaped us, made us who we are today, for good or for bad. But what did we know about our parents' past? Next to nothing. Never asked. Never *dared* to ask, for fear of what might be lurking behind the amiable parental façade.

I didn't want to start an argument with Helmut, and left his rhetorical questions unanswered. In the silence that followed, I turned the page in the scrapbook. My God, there was a wedding photo of my parents that I'd never seen before. Mum in a long white chiffon dress with a modest V-neck, holding a large bunch of white roses; Dad in his grey lieutenant's Nazi uniform sporting various medals. I had no idea, nor did I want to know, what they were for. I can only guess. The newly married couple smiling happily into the camera. In the background, bombed-out houses like burnt-out skeletons, in between empty spaces with piles of bricks and twisted metal. Strange to think that I enjoyed playing in the rubble as a boy, digging for 'treasure'. On the back of the photo, written in pencil: *Our Wedding Day, Köln, 15 July 1944*. Why on earth did they get married during the war? Oh, I see: she was already two months pregnant.

They married five days before the unsuccessful attempt on Hitler's life led by Claus von Stauffenberg. I wondered whether Dad had the slightest inkling that something like that might happen. Surely he must have known the war was all but lost by then, and working as a counter-espionage officer he may well have heard rumours about people in the resistance movement. For a brief moment I imagined him as one of the four conspirators. Brave soldiers. Their bomb plot very nearly succeeded. But then he would have been executed and I would never have been born. I just thought how nice it would have been to be able to say, 'I'm proud of my dad.'

I'm not. I can't even say I know him. *I don't know what you did in the war, Dad. I was always afraid to ask – all of us were – and now it's too late. However, I'm certain the war left deep scars on you – not just physically, but it changed who you once were. And, since you are part of my history, I need to find out more about you. How? Well, we all leave something of ourselves behind when we leave a place and you mentioned some of the places you'd been. I still have my notes of where you were stationed in the war – that's all you ever told me, a list of countries and dates. Something remains there – things we can only discover by going back to those dark places. I have some photos of you now, an old ciné film and hopefully I will find Mum's diary, in which she talks about you. And, of course, there are my own childhood memories, which will help to shed some light on the underdeveloped picture. Unlike Helmut, I don't wish to bury our history and move on. There's something else. I tried to love you, Dad. All my life I tried, and I don't know why I failed.*

'So you haven't found any diaries or anything else where this picture might have come from, then?' I asked Helmut. He glanced at the wedding photo as if acknowledging a familiar item and shrugged his shoulders.

'You can try her bookshelves. They need sorting out too, but be quick. We don't want to be here all day.'

It made me sad to think that most of Mum's neatly arranged books in their mahogany bookcases would soon be relegated to some ramshackle second-hand bookshop. So I placed what I could carry in my suitcase, mainly novels, some of which she'd read to me as a child. And then, just as I thought I'd finished, I caught sight of a purple document wallet right at the top. It contained an article entitled 'Sad and Joyful Events' by Cäcilia Berger, published in *Days of Fear – Senior Citizens Write about the End of the Second World War*. I knew Mum had attended a life writing group, but she'd never mentioned any publications. The same wedding photo I'd found in the scrapbook had been used to illustrate her contribution. The book itself, however, was not on any of the shelves. What a treasure trove of information this would be. I'll read Mum's article tonight, I thought, before visiting her in the care home tomorrow. I slipped the document wallet into the cigar box and resealed it. I'd ask Mum about her diary. Perhaps mentioning *Days of Fear* would jog her memory.

'Do you want any of those photos or not?' Helmut asked, pointing to the shoebox on the coffee table. 'And why are you so obsessed with finding a diary that may no longer exist?'

He paused for a second, then added a word of warning: 'Not always a good place to go, the past – poking around in old papers and photographs, as you do.'

Tempers were frayed enough, so I decided to take the whole shoebox and put it into my case. Then I helped to carry removal boxes into the van Helmut had hired for the occasion.

At this stage I should declare a personal interest. I teach German History at a London university. To be precise, mostly post-war German history. A colleague from the History department and I are jointly writing *Fractured Lives* – a book about the end of the Second World War told from the perspective of ordinary German citizens.

Was it really true that we never talked about the war at home?

Chapter 2

I visited Mum in her new twenty-four-seven care home on Saturday afternoon. It was only my second visit since she'd moved in two months ago, but seeing her new one-room apartment furnished for the first time it looked rather cramped. She was sitting slumped in the only armchair by the window. It smelled musty and the air was stale; the lilies on her bedside table had dropped their petals and lost their delicate fragrance. Her short, grey hair was unkempt. It was early afternoon, and I wondered whether she'd only just got up before I arrived. Like many old people, she used to nap several times during the day, usually fully clothed and wrapped up in a warm duvet. I bent down over her chair to greet her.

'Jonas! What a lovely surprise. I didn't know you were coming to see me,' she beamed, stretching her arms out for an embrace. She tilted her face to receive a kiss. She was wearing some sort of flowery perfume, which seemed to cloud her every movement.

'You look nice.' As usual, she commented on my appearance. I always dress smart-casual when I visit Mum; I wouldn't turn up in an old sweatshirt and jeans like Helmut. She liked the colourful striped shirt I was wearing and was impressed that I hadn't turned grey yet, despite being in my early fifties.

'I've brought you some flowers and some chocolates.' She loves Kinder chocolates, which come individually wrapped in snack bars. As I looked around for a vase, I discovered a large bowl full of her favourite chocolates. I couldn't help laughing.

'You've got enough here to feed an army.'

No response. She probably didn't have her hearing aid in, so I repeated the phrase, slowly and loudly.

'You see,' she said with a fading smile, 'I must have chocolates to offer to my visitors, and now I don't need to worry any more about them being poisoned. Are we in *Köln* now?'

'Hey… What do you mean?' I queried, putting my hand soothingly over hers on the armrest. Her fingers felt warm and soft.

'Well, you know. After the war some American soldiers threw chocolates and sweets in the streets for the children. But we were all under strict orders not to pick them up, because they were assumed to be poisoned.'

Would this be a good moment to talk in more detail about the end of the war, I wondered. Remind her of her contribution to *Days of Fear* and prompt her gently to talk about her diary and ask her what had happened to it?

When I'd arranged the dahlias and chrysanthemums in an oval-shaped glass vase I'd found in her sideboard, I tried cautiously to broach the subject. I lowered my voice to be more persuasive.

'Mum, do you remember—?'

'And how do you like it here?' she interrupted me, sitting up in her armchair. I assured her that I liked her new home and that I was glad that she'd already made some friends there.

'Yes, I wouldn't want to live in an old people's home,' she said with a frown.

The conversation seemed to be going nowhere. Each time I tried to lead her back to the topic of the war, she went off at a tangent, and after a short while would ask me the same question all over again.

'How do you like it here?' Although my response was always the same, uttered with increasing levels of impatience, it seemed to fall on deaf ears. My words simply trickled through the fissures of her short-term memory. Physically she's not in bad shape considering her age. She's eighty-one and, according to the nurses, still shuffles slowly but unaided through the colour-coded corridors, or ambles along the garden path that meanders around the building, looping safely back to the front door of the care home. However, for our outing this afternoon I checked out her Zimmer frame and loaded it into the boot of the car. It was one of those ultra-modern frames on castors, complete with handbrake, shopping basket and even a mini-seat. I'd perched on it a few times, wheeling away the time when I'd visited her in hospital, as there never seemed to be enough chairs for visitors. The hard plastic seat had the surface of a non-stick griddle pan, leaving a ridged imprint on one's bottom if one lingered too long. I never liked sitting on the edge of her hospital bed. I preferred resting on the frame, to avoid getting tangled up in the tubes and risk pulling down her drip.

According to her GP, Mum has 'moderate to severe dementia', meaning she cannot recall things that happened minutes, days, weeks or months ago. However, I'd noticed the occasional lucid flash, when she surprised me with feats of long-term memory, delving into her distant past, uncovering significant details about her life, her family and the days of ruin and hardship before I was born. If only I could gently coax her into talking about the end of the war, and – even more important – get her to tell me where or with whom she'd left her diary …

'Always tidy up your room and you'll never lose things,' she had drummed into us children. Before the move, her flat had been spotless, everything in its place: her French textbook, grammar and vocab book neatly piled up on one side of her desk, her short stories and life writing clearly marked on the other. She even knew the exact location of a book I'd once wanted to borrow, everything was so annoyingly well ordered. But where was her diary? Would she remember? She couldn't even remember what she'd had for breakfast or who had been to visit her the previous day. She didn't remember that she'd almost died in my arms in the hospital a few months ago.

The consultant, a stout, bald-headed man with a slightly harassed manner, had sat me down in a private room and told me in no uncertain terms that there was nothing more they could do for her.

'Almost every organ is damaged, I'm afraid – and her heart is very weak. She doesn't have long to live. Perhaps you should consider transferring her to a hospice.'

The bad news was delivered in an unsympathetic, harsh tone. Miserable git … She's not a bloody write-off yet. He needed the bed for the patients he had temporarily shunted off into the corridors, and they were pleading with him to be moved into one of the three-bedded bays where Mother was occupying an urgently needed space. We disregarded his advice and started to make arrangements for her transfer to a care home.

'You are going to your new home, Mum. Coming out of hospital soon,' I had said.

'That's nice. Where is it?' she perked up, pushing the duvet to one side.

'Soon, not just yet,' I said. 'Justina is going to make you look pretty first.'

The nurse dabbed a bit of blusher on her pale cheeks, and massaged her hands and arms, which had turned purple-black from the numerous times blood had been taken from them. Before moving on to the next patient, she discreetly slipped two incontinence pads into Mother's small travel bag.

The discharge papers weren't ready yet. We were put off until the next day. Somehow old people seem to turn into small children again, I thought, exiting through the revolving door, which turned full circle and stopped automatically in the same place. I was so sad to see that she'd lost any sense of time. She didn't know what time of day it was, nor the day of the week. She had no idea how long she'd been in hospital or how many days we'd kept vigil at her bedside. She floated in and out of timeless space. Only light and darkness regulated her biological clock. Her wristwatch had been packed away in her bedside table, where its futile hands turned round and round, ticking away into the void. How much longer? She survived the tiring journey to her new care home without any difficulty, but again she had no recollection of this. She never looks back, cannot look back any more – not into the recent past, anyway. A blessing or a curse?

We were about to leave her tiny apartment on the

orange-coloured corridor of her care home. I like the print of August Macke's *Lady in Green Jacket* on her door, guiding her back to her room whenever she gets lost. The artist has used warm tones, predominantly orange, green and yellow, and contour lines that outline the five faceless individuals. The lady wearing the green jacket is the only one without a partner. Mum had been on her own for three years – I wondered how much she remembered, or wished to remember, about Dad, who died two days after being admitted to a hospice.

'We're almost ready to go, Mum. Your shoes?' She shuffled forward, sat at the edge of her armchair, bending down to put on her socks. Her naked feet looked like a pair of old worn-out shoes. I knelt down beside her and helped her to slip on her walking boots, which she insisted on wearing.

'Shall we go?' She looked at me as if she had already forgotten about our outing. Her pale blue eyes were weeping slightly under her drooping eyelids. Over the years, the azure blue had been washed away by the trickle of her constantly inflamed eyes. I gently wiped off a couple of droplets that had come to rest on her straight-edged nose. Years of sorrow and sun had etched deep lines into her face, causing her dry skin to lose its elasticity. The old no longer fit their skin – it hangs off them like a room-for-growth jumper. Her life story was buried in those creases and furrows, some of which I was keen to unearth.

Her short piece 'Sad and Joyful Events', although interesting and quite moving, mainly described her wedding under difficult circumstances. What I wanted to find was her diary for 1944, 1945. I thought it would reveal her changing attitude towards the war – perhaps even include a critical evaluation of her leading role in the BdM (*Bund deutscher Mädel* – League of German Girls), the Nazi youth movement. Or would she be in denial to the bitter end of the war? … But I didn't want to ask her that. I needed to tread carefully.

'Have you told the nurse I am taking you out for a walk this afternoon?' I asked her.

'Take out what?' she replied.

'We are going for a walk. Have you told the nurse?' I repeated, raising my voice. She tilted her head slightly to the left and looked up to the ceiling trying to remember.

'I don't know.'

'Never mind. I'll tell her on our way out.'

'How do you like it here?' she asked me again on our way to the car park.

'I feel at home where I am.' A deliberately ambiguous response. I knew what she'd have liked to hear, some kind of 'I'd like to come home to the fatherland', a hint of longing to live near the family rather than in my 'English exile', as she used to call it. 'The prodigal son is not coming home, Mum.' But I didn't tell her that.

'We'll take the car to the rec, and on the way back we'll stop somewhere for coffee.' I tried to enunciate my words as clearly as possible, speaking slowly and loudly, since I wasn't sure whether she was wearing her hearing aid.

'You've wrecked the car?' she said anxiously, lowering herself down slowly on to the passenger seat. OK. No hearing aid.

'We are driving to the recreation ground first, then we'll stop off for a cup of coffee and some cake,' I shouted back at her. I needed to find her hearing aid before we left. I went back to her room, riffled through her bedside table drawers, and eventually found the two plastic earpieces hidden beneath her pillow. She let me fit them in her ears, where they sat snugly like baby snails and, due to their nude skin-like tone, were barely visible. Is there anything to be said in favour of the onset of deafness? Any heightening of other senses? A feeling of going to a quieter, lonelier place? I don't know.

We eventually sat down in an almost empty café after an excruciatingly slow walk on the rec with frequent stops and starts. Mother repeated her favourite question, this time with a rhetorical tag and in a much lower tone, since she could now hear again:

'So how do you like it here? I suppose you don't want to come home again.'

Fortunately, the waiter arrived before I had time to reply. Saved by the cheesecake! While she tucked in with gusto, I considered how best to broach the subject of her distant past under the Nazis, hoping to tease out an eyewitness account of the end of the war. My pretext was not a particularly subtle one, but seemed to do the trick.

'I looked at your life writing in 'Senior Citizens Write about the End of the Second World War'... Do you remember anything about your contribution? Bits and pieces you reconstructed from your diary, maybe?'

'Diary?' she repeated, like an actor who has to be prompted for the next line. 'My mother didn't approve of me writing a diary. She scolded me for raving about the BdM and confiscated my diary when I was just ten. I was only a child when I joined. All my friends did. But she kept it and gave it back to me before she died. It's still at home.'

'And what about your war diary?' She looked at me in disbelief. *Is he serious?* She put her cake fork down, sat back in her chair, tilting her head in thought and started to turn her wedding ring with thumb and middle finger, as if to conjure up vivid images from the past.

'Those were hard times, you know – unimaginably hard times. But there were happy events, too. Dad and I got married in July 1944 – we were both allowed two days' special leave from military service on the Eastern Front.'

'How on earth was it possible to arrange a wedding in the midst of war?' I asked, encouraging her to continue.

'It wasn't easy. I don't know how they did it, but my parents managed to organise such a lovely wedding for us.' She paused again with a faint smile, then sighed disconcertingly. 'Our flat in *Köln* was bombed out twice – we lost almost everything. We had to move to my uncle's flat. The night before the wedding, we took refuge in the air-raid shelter, listening to the endless firebombs hitting houses nearby.'

She covered one ear as if to protect herself from the blasts, paused, gasped for breath and dug deeper into her past. Her face turned alarmingly red, then her left hand began to shake.

'I can still hear the screams of the injured and those buried in the rubble – mothers and children crying for help in the raging fire storm. Elsa, our neighbour who shared the shelter with us, suddenly grabbed my arm and started shouting: "Cäcilia, uncle Ernst is burning to death – someone help him!"'

The left side of Mum's face seemed to have drooped; her speech began to slur.

'Are you OK, Mum? Can you hear me? Mum?' She slumped back in her chair and didn't stir. When the ambulance arrived ten minutes later, the paramedic asked her to raise her left arm – she couldn't. He explained what I had already feared: she'd suffered a stroke.

'Whatever brought this on?' Helmut asked when he joined me in hospital an hour later. He sat bolt upright on the edge of his chair in the visitors' room, shredding a paper tissue into little pieces with his hands while asking the consultant more questions about the ensuing treatment. Apparently she'd had a mini-stroke about six months ago, the doctor told us, which had shown up on the CT scan. He explained that this time Mum had suffered an ischaemic stroke, caused by a blood clot obstructing the flow of blood to the brain. However, since there was no bleeding in and around the brain, she would have a good chance of making a full recovery. I breathed a sigh of relief, which must have been audible, since Helmut gave me a probing look as if he were cross-examining a court witness. He's a judge, and for a short moment I imagined myself sitting in the dock before him being accused of grievous bodily harm: 'Did you not think that encouraging mother to relive those terrifying moments towards the end of the war was likely to have a devastating effect on her health and could lead to her premature death?'

I listened to myself with the guilty conscience of a voyeur, and only snapped out of the imagined court case when Helmut reminded me that Mum would need her things from the care home. I volunteered to return there and pack a bag for her time in hospital.

'My mother didn't approve of me writing a diary.' Mum's phrase lingered in my mind as I drove back to the home. Was it really true that she'd kept her childhood diary? And, more importantly, if there was a war diary it might have travelled with her to her new home after all.

I was used to trawling through library microfiches for historical records, but rummaging through Mum's personal things didn't feel right. However, I didn't have to search for long. Top drawer of her sideboard: amongst a pile of correspondence, opened letters and holiday postcards, a brown envelope stood out bearing the single word, *Cäcilia*, in Sütterlin script. Inside were three pages of a child's diary in neat handwriting, written in blue ink on sheets of paper torn from a school exercise book – the most beautiful handwriting you could imagine, with all the letters carefully staying within the lines. I could feel my heart pounding as I began to read.

24 October 1933

I'm so happy today. It's two weeks after my 10th birthday and I passed the entry test for the BdM. Running 60 metres under 12 seconds was really difficult but I just managed it. Long jump and throwing a ball were OK. I haven't told Mum about it. She doesn't like me joining the BdM one bit. She said she hates the brown party. 'Up to no good they are,' she said, 'stay away from them.' She is a Social Democrat – don't really know what that means. She won't buy me the uniform and I can't join without it. Now I'm sad again and don't know what to do. All my friends have

*joined and I don't want to be the odd one out. When I
said 'Everyone is joining in my class', she just said 'We
don't do what everyone does, basta.' So annoying.*

25 October
*I went to ask Dad and he bought me the uniform.
Yeah! I tried it on. It looks amazing: a white blouse
with two pockets in the front and a dark blue pleated
skirt. Embroidered on the left upper arm of the blouse
there is the diamond-shaped swastika on a red–white
background. We are told to wear long white socks and
brown shoes with our uniform. I proudly showed my
girlfriends this afternoon.*

28 October
*After school I went to the official joining ceremony.
There was a long speech about the Führer which I
didn't really understand, and then all the new girls
were awarded the black neckerchief and plaited leather
woggle. From now on I'm officially allowed to wear
the BdM uniform. Also, we all had to swear an oath
of allegiance to the Führer: 'I hereby swear that I shall
always do my duty in the Hitler Youth in love and
faith to the Führer and to our flag, so help me God.'*

3 November
*Mum won't wash or iron my uniform, that's so
annoying. I can't turn up in a dirty uniform. We get
inspected every week by our BdM leader. She says
everything must be tidy and clean or we are sent home
straight away. I asked Grandma to wash it for me and*

now Mum is cross with her too. Our BdM leader is
called Wiebke Thron. She always looks very smart. She
talked to us about the different ranks, in case any of
us wants to become a leader one day. We had to draw
different colour ribbons and write the rank next to it:
Red-White striped ribbon – Schaftführerin (leader of a
group of up to 15 girls)
Green-White – Scharführerin (leader of a group of up
to 45 girls)
White – Ringführerin (leader of a group of up to 60
girls)
Blue – Bannmädelführerin (leader of a group of up to
75 girls)
The top rank (blue) is like a full-time job, she said.

9 November

We have meetings once a week. We meet at the
Volksgarten and learn to march two by two to the
sports ground. I was allowed to carry the flag for the
first time. We do lots of different sports, which is great,
and I'm getting better at long jump. Sometimes we
have a lesson like at school where we have to sit still
for an hour and learn about obedience, faithfulness and
decency. It's so boring. But then we sing a song at the
end – and that's nice. Today we were given the second
verse to learn for next week:

Uns're Fahne flattert uns voran
Our flag is flying in front of us
Uns're Fahne ist die neue Zeit
Our flag is the new age
Und die Fahne führt uns in die Ewigkeit

And the flag leads us into eternity
Ja, die Fahne ist mehr als der Tod.
Yes, our flag means more than death.

12 November
Damn. Mum has snooped around my room and found my diary. She is VERY angry!!! I'm grounded for a whole week. And she wants me to stop writing 'your silly diary about the BdM' and concentrate on my schoolwork. And she's told Dad not to buy me a BdM climbing jacket for Christmas. So what am I going to wear with my uniform in the winter?

Good old socialist Grandma. She obviously sussed it right from the start: nicely disguised post-school activities with an indoctrinating propaganda twist. I wondered whether Mother had listened to Hitler's Nuremberg speech on the radio, two years after she'd joined the BdM in 1935, in which he proclaimed his 'educational objectives' in front of a crowd of 50,000 Hitler Youth: 'the German youth has to be lithe and lissom, as fast as greyhounds, tough as leather, and hard as Krupp steel.'

There was no trace of her war diary in the care home. I'd just packed Mum's hospital bag with some toiletries and a couple of magazines when I noticed that I still had her old flat key in my pocket.

Chapter 3

As I turned the key to unlock Mum's flat on Sunday morning, I felt like an intruder. I don't know why I wanted to go inside one last time. Maybe it was to say goodbye to lots of happy memories: when Mum was still in possession of all her faculties, when we talked for hours about books we had read and the ones we were writing or wanted to write. She sometimes read to me from her collection of stories, which she had called *Serene and Reflective Moments*. They consisted mostly of short diary entries about humorous things we had said or done as children, which always made us laugh. We never tired of hearing them again and again.

Now, the sense of togetherness, of a shared life, had suddenly evaporated into the ether. The mother I had known was no more. I felt utterly bereft. As I sat slumped over her desk, head cupped in my hands, eyes closed, I could hear her sing 'Brahms' Lullaby' to me at my bedside:

Good evening, good night,
With roses covered,
With cloves adorned,
Slip under the covers.
Tomorrow morning, if God wills,
You will wake once again.

'Good night, sleep tight,' she used to say, tucking me in and kissing me gently on the forehead. Were these the earliest memories of my mother? The feeling of her hands, the sound of her voice and the scent of her hair? I don't know. I just wanted to wrap myself in the cloak of my remembered world and be safe in it for a while. Gradually the memories receded. I became aware of my awkward posture, sat up and looked around. There was nothing left in the flat, except for some lifeless furniture. The mahogany bookcases, the rosewood table and chairs and the antique pedestal desk with its leather skiver top – all to be auctioned to the highest bidder. 'They should fetch a few bob,' Helmut had said. I didn't care. I got up and walked round the room, opening empty drawers and staring at the bare bookshelves. It felt as if all the blood had been drained out of the flat and all that was left was a decomposing corpse.

Furniture Auction, the sign had read in my grandparents' front garden. I must have been seven or eight years old when Dad had been desperate to buy back some of the furniture that had been claimed by the bailiff. Grandad, once an affluent businessman who'd owned several machine tool factories, had lost everything in the war, but still had to pay off his creditors. Hence the huge house, furniture, car – everything – came under the hammer. Dad had never talked much about his father, other than that he was very strict, and had punished and beaten him and his brother when they had misbehaved. He also made them do their military service before they were allowed to study.

Initially, Dad was also looking to see whether there were any items that didn't have the bailiff's seal stuck underneath, colloquially called *Kuckuck*. An amusing name, I thought. So I skipped along the parquet floors, making cuckoo noises that echoed round the half-empty rooms.

'Will you stop that – immediately!' he shouted at me, as he was adding up what he could afford to buy back. It was years later, when we moved to a new house, that I realised he'd bought back much of their antique Chippendale furniture, which looked very old-fashioned to us children.

I wondered for a moment whether any of the furniture in Mum's flat had originally come from Grandad's house. Now that all pieces were 'cuckoo-free', none of us wanted them.

I locked up and took Mum's keys downstairs to the warden, a handsome middle-aged woman with a gentle lined face on which small dabs of rouge were visible in little patches on her cheekbones. She seemed friendly and was quite chatty.

'And how's your mother?' she asked, as I handed her the keys. 'Does she like her new home? I guess it's very different from living independently here at Vivat. She's a lovely woman, your mum. And so clever. All that creative writing and encouraging her friends to join the group. Even some of the men went. Great inspiration, she was. We do so miss her here.'

'Yes, she's very well, thank you.' I didn't want to tell her she'd suffered a stroke.

'You mentioned the creative writing class. Did you ever see the book they published? I think it was called *Days of Fear*? You wouldn't have a copy by any chance, would you?'

'Gosh, that was some time ago. I don't think I ever saw a copy of the book. Sorry. I tell you what, though. Her best friend, Elsa Kohl – she'd certainly have a copy. But she moved away last year – to live with her niece, I think.'

Sadly, two of your mother's fellow writers died last year. Such a shame.'

She paused for thought, then got up and glanced at the noticeboard to check the list of current residents.

'Ah, there's Frau Schuhmacher, on the ground floor. She's still here, and I believe she was one of the authors. You could talk to her. Would you like me to give her a ring? See if you could have a word with her?'

Half an hour later Frau Schumacher was chatting away to me about her contribution to the book. A plump, grey-haired woman, she was probably about my mother's age, with pale cheeks and dark brown eyes. These were underscored by shadows – not shadows of weariness, exhaustion or illness, but of seriousness and melancholy. When she'd satisfied her curiosity about Mum's new home, Frau Schuhmacher explained to me that she'd given the book to her daughter for safe keeping. 'You know,' she said, 'it's important for the younger generation to learn what it was like during the war, and you won't find this kind of story in the history books.'

I couldn't agree more. A people's history, history 'from the bottom up', reconstructing the experiences of ordinary people, was exactly the type of narrative that interested me. I was seeking eyewitness accounts of historical events rather than regurgitated narratives emphasising single great or evil historical figures.

'I can remember the gist of the story I wrote,' she began, 'but may have forgotten some of the details. That's why we wrote them down – so our children and their children can read them when we are no longer here.' She sipped at her coffee, leaned back in her armchair, hands folded on her lap, and began to tell her story as if reading it from a book.

'During the war, we used to live on a small farm in Premnitz in Eastern Germany, and on the farm next to us they employed a few forced labourers and prisoners of war from Russia and Poland, who helped in the fields and fed the animals. The farmer's wife treated them very badly and gave them very little to eat. One day she discovered a small piece of smoked ham under the mattress of a young Russian prisoner – Roman can't have been older than about seventeen at the time. As a punishment, they let him starve, tied up in the stables for three days, poor chap. We felt sorry for him and nursed him back to health. On Sundays he used to come round to play with us children, and my mother gave him food and tobacco.'

'How old were you then?' I interrupted.

'I was only ten years old when the war ended in May 1945. All of a sudden everything changed from one day to the next. The forced labourers and prisoners of war were free, but there was barely any food for them. So they formed gangs, got hold of weapons and ammunition, and then took revenge on their former employers. They roamed the countryside, stealing cows, pigs and chickens. Anybody who tried to resist them was shot. When they came to our farm, trying to take our cows, my mother barred their way to the cowshed, despite having a revolver pointed at her. I was really frightened.

'All of a sudden Roman emerged from the gang. "These are good people. They helped me when I was ill – leave them alone!" he shouted to his comrades, and thankfully they left us in peace. Afterwards, I always jumped whenever

I heard a knock on the door, but mostly they were scruffy-looking ex-soldiers begging for a bowl of soup.'

I had obviously overestimated Frau Schuhmacher's age, for she was a lot younger than my mother, and her account had been a story handed down by her parents. Hers was a narrative retold and filtered through the eyes of a child, loyal and keen to maintain the good name of the family: 'Others were cruel; we were kind.' It was one of the many 'perpetrators became victims' stories, without any information about the role her parents played in the war – a feel-good story for the next generation.

I had heard similar accounts from my classmates at grammar school, in which loving fathers who were Nazi sympathisers somehow turned into heroic resistance fighters. Stories about people who pleaded ignorance or didn't ask any questions when their Jewish schoolmates disappeared from one day to the next. They had simply 'emigrated to America'. Like second-hand clothes, handed-down memories lose their shape over time and can stretch beyond recognition. For those who lived through the war, memories fade and reminders may be needed. Sometimes these prompts are understandably rejected by tormented souls or, as in Mum's case, can cause a person to relive some of their horrific experiences. Sorry, Mum. 'Not always a good idea to delve too deeply into someone's past,' Helmut had warned me when he handed me my cigar box of memorabilia.

But I wanted to talk to the last eyewitnesses, hear and read their accounts, understand their actions by piecing together the many sources into something that made sense to me. My inherited cigar box had now provided me with a number of authentic sources, some of which I needed to research further, like my Dad's film roll and stacks of photos and Mum's diary extract. These would help me to fill in gaps and answer questions I had never asked. They were snapshots of real history, capturing the atmosphere and the zeitgeist, and, most important of all, they would reveal something about their past I was eager to know.

Before leaving Frau Schuhmacher, I wanted to ask her if she knew of Elsa Kohl's whereabouts. If Elsa really had been my mother's best friend, she would maybe know what happened to her war diary and whether it still existed. But I was surprised at her frosty reaction.

'I know she was a friend of your mother's, but we didn't like her. Her story didn't get published. She left the group early on and moved abroad. I think she went to live with her niece in London. Elsa said she'd send us a postcard, but we never heard a word from her. I'm not surprised.'

Would I be able to find Elsa's name in the London telephone directory, or would she have changed her name? If she was living with her niece, the entry would be in her niece's name. I needed to find her, but how?

That evening, when I said my goodbyes to Mum, Helmut sat by her bedside in hospital, and I was glad to see that she had recovered somewhat.

I arrived back in London on Sunday night, still smarting at having been fined £30 for excess luggage, despite my best efforts to cram as many books and pieces of memorabilia as possible into my hand luggage. And it didn't help coming back to an empty, cold Victorian house that was in urgent need of redecoration. Strangely enough, whenever

I'd been away for a few days, I returned to my house like a curious observer. I often wondered what kind of statement my house makes about me. It's an old place, covered by an unruly red Virginia creeper, which I quite like. When my ex-wife Lucy was still living with me, she had it cut back every three months so that it would attract fewer spiders. Well, that was the reason she gave for the trim. Had I not put my foot down, she would have replaced all of the draughty sash windows with new PVC ones. She even favoured replacing the old fireplace and the solid oak front door, with its cast-iron facings. Admittedly, the door groans and grates against the stone floor, but that's part of the attraction of an old house, isn't it? Imagine – it must once have been in the habit of shutting behind you with a sonorous bang. As you stepped inside, you were greeted with the sound of two grandfather clocks ticking out of sync, the vibrant colours and textures of the original wallpaper, beginning to peel here and there, and the slightly musty odour as you entered the living room.

It was here and in the bedroom that Lucy had stamped her feminine signature. The fireplace and the shelves were smothered with ornaments and useless nick-knacks. Looking back on it, I think the objects themselves had always suggested promiscuous sexuality: the cocks and hens, the nymphs and lovebirds and the frenzied pair of cockatoos. I'm not sure why I'd been reluctant to remove the offending items once she had left me to move in with her longstanding lover, who could keep her in the style to which she had become accustomed from her nouveau riche upbringing. Maybe there's a link between vulgarity, wealth and female sexuality. I should have suggested it as a research topic to colleagues in the Sociology department.

The Ten o'clock News was very depressing. One year after the invasion of Iraq, there were still car bombs and suicide attacks killing innocent civilians on an almost daily basis. Unlike in post-war Germany, the Allies didn't seem to have any plans or strategies for dealing with the aftermath of the war. Hailed as liberators in Germany in 1945, in today's Iraq they are infamous for war crimes – the horrific pictures of torture in Abu Ghraib prison still haunt me. How ironic that the news ended with an item on Simon Wiesenthal, Holocaust survivor, who was being awarded an honorary knighthood in recognition of a lifetime of service to humanity for bringing Nazi war criminals to justice.

Once unpacked, I took the whole of my 'inheritance' upstairs, placed the items in a corner of my study without a single backward glance and went to bed. I was exhausted but lay there for ages unable to sleep, as my mind was scrutinising the different items contained in the cigar box. Each object, like exhibits in a court case, would be physical evidence connected with a particular event. The innocent items from my childhood would evoke distinct memories, but how accurate would they be? Or would I just use them to spin a good yarn? I'd need to give other exhibits – such as the ciné film roll, old photos, the undeveloped 35mm film roll and the diary entries – some forensic treatment in order to reconstruct my parents' lives, and describe the people, places and events to which they were connected.

In the middle of the night, as if attacked by a ravenous appetite, I woke up overcome by the desire to open up the past again, and once more examine in detail some of the 'treasures' my parents had bequeathed me. I'd hoped that all of the evils had flown out of Pandora's box (Pandora's was actually a large jar), leaving only pleasant memorabilia inside. I turned on my bedside lamp, fetched the box from the study and ripped off the brown packaging seal. I wasn't sure why, but I began by fishing out all the toys, one by one. Everything else would have to wait until the morning. Strange – there was one toy I hadn't noticed before: a small, wooden arrow, about ten centimetres long with a rubber sucker at one end. As I touched it, I experienced a mental lurch of memory …

I was a short-trousered schoolboy again, coming home in the late afternoon, socks round my ankles, knees scuffed from playing in the ruins with my toy rifle. Front-loaded with the wooden arrow, it would have had a range of four to five metres and would stick to windows or smooth ceilings, leaving a circular mark (or worse) when aimed at flies. Dad had bought it secretly for my sixth birthday, and I was supposed to hide it in the cellar before going upstairs. I remembered the rather harsh reception from Mum when I turned up, still carrying it in my arms.

'Why are you playing outside in your school trousers? Why didn't you change?' She slapped at them with her hand.

'And who on earth gave you that rifle? I don't want you to play with that ever again.'

'But Dad said I could–'

'And I say put it away for good, or I will.'

'Muuummm …'

She stood up tall with a no-nonsense look on her face

as if to say, 'Don't even think about asking Dad …', shook her head in despair and bent down again.

'What a sight you are! Just look at your face!' She pulled a handkerchief out of her sleeve, spat on it and rubbed my cheeks.

'Don't, Mum!' I hated it when she did that and I just wanted to run off, but I then had some urgent questions to ask her. I had spotted some British soldiers outside the house and wanted to know what they were doing here.

'Mum, how long will those soldiers stay in our town? Is there going to be another war?'

'I don't know. They'll be here for a while, until things are back to normal, and no, the war is definitely over now.'

'Grandma said we are back to normal now. She said you can buy bananas and oranges in the market. She also told me we don't have to scrimp on butter any more.'

'Yes, we're almost back to normal now.'

'Helmut said there are there still German prisoners of war coming back from Russia, but you said the war was over a long time ago. So why are they coming back now?'

'Goodness, you do ask some odd questions. I suppose it takes time to sort things out. Now – go and take those filthy trousers off. And don't just leave them on the floor!'

All I knew as a six-year-old was that something very bad had happened in the past, something that nobody wished to talk about. I had no conception of war and destruction on an unimaginable scale. To me it wasn't obvious that things weren't normal at that time. Perhaps I had some strange fascination with the eerie landscape of bombed-out houses and flattened rectangular spaces, interspersed with huge craters filled with brown water. For us children these spaces meant adventure playgrounds, places to hide and create an ambush. We resented the bulldozers clearing one site after another. Usually, when they had torn everything down, a group of people, mostly women, would start to clean the bricks salvaged from the rubble of the knocked-down houses and pile them up in an orderly fashion. Occasionally, after dusk we would go and nick a few bricks to build mini observation towers with arrow slits from which to launch an attack on the unsuspecting enemy. There we were, boys playing soldiers in the rubble with wooden swords and clubs and toy guns, stabbing and shooting at one another, re-enacting scenes from a war we knew little about.

However many questions we asked about the war, nobody wanted to explain to us children what had happened. There'd been a war and that was that. Now we would just have to roll up our sleeves, work hard and start again from scratch.

Yet, there were daily reminders of the recent past, which threw up new questions I was curious about and sought answers to. St Vinzenz Hospital, which specialised in caring for war veterans, was only a few streets away from where we lived. Mum told me that the doctors did a great job helping ex-soldiers to walk again by using artificial limbs and by mending the skins of airmen who had been severely burnt in air crashes. But whenever we met a one-legged man on crutches, my mum grabbed my hand and hurried past. She said it was rude to stare at these poor people, but to me it seemed equally rude to hurry past and look the other way. I really didn't know what to do and often wondered what these men would have preferred.

At home I practised walking with Grandma's crutches, pretending to have lost a leg. I thought of all the things I would no longer be able to do if I had only one leg. A few days later, I saw a man in the street whose right arm was missing below the elbow; the sleeve of his coat was neatly pinned back to his chest. When I looked at him and said 'Hello', he doffed his broad-rimmed hat and smiled.

I finally fell into a deep sleep after this mental excursion into my early childhood. I dreamed Dad was still alive, telling me how he got injured by a grenade that killed his comrades in the trench next to him. I put my arm round him as he sobbed. I don't recall Dad ever talking to me about this, or did he? Helmut must have told me about it. That morning, I wrote 'Photos' on my to-do list. I wanted to get the old film roll developed and find out whether they could transfer Dad's ciné film on to DVD, so I could watch it at home. I looked at my wall calendar: 27 September – one more week until the start of the new term, preparation for my lecture series on post-war Germany and a few errands to run.

Chapter 4

Monday morning. I'd set the alarm for seven thirty and clumsily swiped the film roll off the bedside table when reaching for the snooze button. I'd put it there to remind me to take it to the photographer's shop.

It was still puzzling me when I stepped into the shower. Why would Dad have left behind an undeveloped film roll, nor bothered to show us the old ciné film? If there were things he didn't want us to see, he could have destroyed the evidence. Had he wanted me to find them after his death? And how did these items end up in my cigar box, alongside innocent relics from my childhood? It didn't make much sense to me. He could easily have developed the film himself, in the privacy of the darkroom in his shop.

Let me call him to mind, then, just after the war. His new career was taking off, with the opening of his first shop opposite the town's savings bank. At the time, Rudolf Berger had been a soldier for eight long years. First he was enrolled for compulsory military service from 1937 to 1939, and then – we think – he served in the Wehrmacht as a counter-espionage officer. His official title, however, was Signal Corps Officer. Although he was allowed to study Medicine for almost five terms in 1939, 1940, the ensuing war prevented him from gaining any professional qualification. In the summer of 1945 – broke, and in desperate need of money to support his new family – he started up a photography business. A couple of pictures in the shoebox I'd picked up from Mum's old flat showed his corner shop with two large dual-aspect windows – one displaying a few cameras, a slide projector and a couple of accessories, all with tiny price tags attached; the other, advertising his portrait photography, sported pictures of happy smiley families with babies and dogs, newlyweds, bride and groom holding hands and exuding joy all over the canvas.

I often dropped into the shop on the way back from school, hoping to earn a bit of extra pocket money by helping out with the odd job. As you stepped inside, opposite each window were wall-to-wall shelves housing more cameras, and photography goods spread out between picture frames to give the impression of a well-stocked glass cabinet. Two old-fashioned cash registers sat on each of the sales counters, making a strange ka-*ching* sound each time Dad opened the till. The back door led to a photo studio equipped with softbox studio lighting, which looked like two oversized umbrellas decked with silver reflectors. In the middle of them, covered by a black linen cloth, stood a bulky camera on a wooden tripod. A few metres away from the camera, on makeshift wooden scaffolding, hung several canvas backdrops in different pastel shades.

'Why is everything upside down?' I once asked Dad when peering through the aperture of the camera as he was about to polish its lens with a lint-free duster.

'Because the aperture is very small, it refracts the light, bending it in a way that inverts the image. It's not just upside down,' he added, 'but it also reverses the image.' He went on to explain the optical characteristics of convex and concave lenses, talked about wide-angle lenses, exposure times, and all that technical stuff.

I can't remember a great deal about my first camera, or the first momentous click of the shutter that was supposed to instil a love of photography in me. I was only ten years old, but even as an adult I found taking photos so cumbersome, having to load the film into the camera without ripping the perforated edge, closing the lid and winding the film on until '1' appeared in the minute dial window and, finally, setting the shutter speed and the distance. What a kerfuffle – all before you'd even taken your first picture. I got bored and lost interest in the whole photography business. However, I have to admit it was fascinating to watch my father perform his magic in the darkroom, although I never quite understood the science behind it.

As soon as you entered the 'laboratory' – Dad always wore his white linen coat and made me wear an apron – the fixer and developer baths' acrid ammonia smell wafted towards you. Most of what was going on in there remained as dark as part of the developing process: apparently, the first steps of taking the film out of its metal drum, cutting both ends off and putting it into the developer bath, had to be done in complete darkness. Then there were different tanks the film had to be bathed in, but I was really only interested in the last stage, where a dim red light could be switched on. Dad would hand me a steel spring clip to hang the negatives up on a rail to dry. Half an hour later the real magic would begin. He exposed each negative on a light-sensitive photographic paper, which in turn would be submerged into the developer bath. I was allowed to carefully dip the paper into the developer with a pair of metal tongs. I can still hear the sound of the liquid, gently lapping as I bathed the paper and watched the image miraculously appear. Amazing!

Afterwards, if I remember correctly, the photographs had to be dipped into a few more baths, filled with various smelly chemicals (was it developer or fixer bath?). I probably haven't got this quite right and Dad would shake his head hearing me explain this. Great fun, though, despite the smell.

As we stepped out of the darkroom, I would take off my apron. When Dad hung up his white linen coat, it felt like he'd simultaneously suspended all his aspirations to become a medical doctor. He wouldn't have looked out of place in a medical practice: he was a handsome man, with clean-cut face, a tanned complexion and black hair combed straight back from his forehead. But he wore the expression of a man whose inner peace had been disturbed. Above his rimless spectacles, there was a constant worry line on his forehead and his eyes looked sad. He was driven, charismatic and compelling, a workaholic with a rare smile. Like an actor, he could blandish, charm or intimidate, sometimes in quick succession.

At work, everything had to be just so. I felt his eager eye on me as I helped him to sort customers' photos, assembling them into wallets – prints in one pocket, negatives in the other. I would then label the wallets with the customer's name and store them alphabetically in the drawer under the counter.

'Come on. You need to work faster if we're going to

get through this lot before dinner,' he used to spur me on, whenever I took my time glancing at people's snaps. There was always the odd photograph that just made me stop and stare. Sometimes a photo's subject is so powerful that it doesn't matter whether it was taken by an amateur or a professional photographer; they capture moments we would like to last. Moments of happiness, reflection or sadness, and any number of other emotions. Why do we have this desire to capture life-memories we would otherwise forget? Children at different stages in their lives, birthdays, weddings – life's big events – all in a single click. For me, pictures tell stories, personal stories. They give you a chance to dream and imagine what it would have been like to be there – just by looking at the image, the space, the background. Letting your mind float and make connections between things.

That's what I wanted to do with my dad's pictures from the undeveloped film roll: make connections, let the images speak to me, imagine the scenes of a life in which I had no part. Would they connect with the person I knew?

I went downstairs for some toast and a cup of tea. Then I delved again into the shoebox full of old, mostly black-and-white photos in order to find the person I thought I knew. Here he was in his forties, a rare glimpse of the man who hardly ever took time off work, who hardly ever rested, checked shirt, baggy trousers held up by tight braces, sitting at the piano. My father, the musician. Pounding the keyboard. I could hear him loud and fast. He had a limited repertoire, like someone who never had the time to learn things properly but who wanted to impress and entertain. He always finished with a Prelude by Chopin – No. 4 in E minor, which is a rather melancholy piece, and for a long time I wrongly associated it with Beethoven, simply because a painting of Beethoven's forlorn expression hung over the piano in a heavy black frame. It was a piece quite unlike his usual repertoire, soft and thoughtful. Sometimes I would stop and listen in awe, watching my father gaze pensively at the empty music stand before him, lost in a different world.

Mother always found fault with his playing – a note that didn't sound quite right. She tried in vain to encourage him to sight-read and study the music. When she practised, she meticulously went over the same phrases again and again; every bar had to be just so. The music score dictated her playing. She would repeat a piece, often with a metronome, until it sounded absolutely perfect – technically, that is. 'The music lacks expression,' Dad would retort. All family members had to learn an instrument – violin, guitar, piano. Mum loved her *Hausmusik*. 'It unites the family', she used to say, and for a short period of time we were all in sync.

Almost all the photos in the shoebox had old-fashioned deckle edges, a rough serrated border (*Büttenrand*). Dad had taught me to ask the customers, '*Mit oder ohne Büttenrand?*' I fished out another photo from the same era: Dad, the gardener, pitchfork in his hands, turning over the heavy soil, removing any wild plant that dared to grow in an unwanted place, especially where it prevented the cultivated plants from growing freely. Did they need more living space? Saturday afternoon was weeding time, and we all had to muck in with two hours' work before we were allowed to go out. How we hated it. He would carry on when we had stopped. Gardening for hours on end until it was dark.

One morning, I recall with a great deal of schadenfreude, our garden had been invaded. Above ground, in the newly sown lawn, were all the tell-tale marks of unsightly molehills: mounds of soil and grassless brown streaks. I remember it well. In fact, there is another photo of him, leaning on the spade with an angry face, pondering his next move, planning his assault on the little creatures. What came next scared and disgusted me: I watched him remove the molehill earth with his spade, which gave a gasp at each contact with the brown soil. He then inserted small gas pellets into the tunnel below and covered up the hole, watered it and waited for the pellets to explode so that the gas would seep into the mole's burrow. I felt sorry for the poor little creatures that had to die in such a horrid way. Later in my life, I made the connection.

I was just about to put the lid back on the shoebox when I caught a glimpse of a photo of Dad and me that suggested rare closeness. I must have been eight or nine, sitting on his right knee, for his left thigh had always been bandaged – a war wound that wouldn't heal. We were both focusing on what seemed to be some kind of puzzle. On closer inspection, with the aid of a magnifying glass, I recognised a square paper grid, complete with individual jumbled-up letters. In his right hand he held another grid, of the same size, which had a number of squares cut out at random. I searched my memory and travelled back to the time when he taught me simple code-making. I tried it out on my friends in class, writing secret messages that could only be read with a key – the paper grid with the cut-out squares. You wrote your message into the spaces occupied by those squares, turned it clockwise several times, depending on the length of the message, and then simply filled the whole grid with random letters so that the code word would magically 'disappear'.

For a short time I became the school's recognised authority on code-making. I even made a little bit of money out of it, charging a few *Pfennige* at a time for a grid with a key. Helmut was very scathing about it, saying it was kids', stuff, and told me Dad had shown him the Enigma-decryption techniques they'd used during the war. I had no idea what he was referring to until much later on. He seemed to have gleaned a lot more about Dad, without letting me in on whatever he knew. Why didn't he want to share this with me? It didn't matter who knew what at a certain point in time. I was convinced I would catch up with him one day.

I'd sent Dad's film roll off for processing and taken the ciné film to the photographer's; both would assist me in developing the past. Strange word, 'develop'. I looked it up in the dictionary. Apparently we borrowed it from the French *développer*, old French *des* + *voloper*, meaning 'to unfold', 'to change the form (of a surface) by bending'. Would the photos and the film allow me to unfold the story that lay behind them; let me make the right connections? Or would I be bending the truth with my own interpretation? I'd have to wait at least a week or two to find out. Would the photos have faded beyond recognition? Was there any technical reason why the old ciné film couldn't be transferred on to DVD?

I sat down at my desk and switched on my computer. Time to prepare my lectures for the next term: 'Postwar German History 1945–1990'. I could do what I had always done, and use timelines and structure the lectures chronologically: 1945 – 'Zero Hour' and the Potsdam Agreement; 1948 – Currency Reform and Berlin Blockade; 1949 – Foundation of the FRG and the GDR, and so on. But this time I wanted to try out something different: teach my students history through telling stories, get them to hear and read eyewitness accounts, make them see and experience what it was like to have actually been there. A 'through their eyes' narrative is what I wanted to present; the facts and figures could go into a handout. A proper historical narrative is not learned parrot-fashion, but is constructed from evidence, from sources, photos, films and documentaries. I wanted to present the historical narrative in the form of an argument and let my students form their own opinions. History is no longer just written by the victors, Mr Churchill. I was thinking how fascinating and motivating it would be for them if I could add my own sources to the teaching materials – another pressing reason why I needed to find Mum's diary and *Days of Fear – Senior Citizens Write About the End of the Second World War*.

Chapter 5

October 2004. The new term had started. I'd settled into my teaching and research routine: preparing handouts with lecture topics, plus reading lists and seminar topics for the students to choose from. I drew their attention to a guest lecture by my colleague, Sam Beckhard, on Goldhagen's view that the vast majority of ordinary Germans were 'willing executioners', an idea that stoked a heated and mostly scathing debate among German and American historians. I decided to prepare my students for the discussion by giving them excerpts from Christopher Browning's *Ordinary Men*, in particular his reply to Goldhagen.

Two weeks had passed since I had taken the ciné film and film roll to the photographer's. I sensed no urgency. Although normally I follow things up swiftly, on this occasion it didn't bother me that they had not called. Had I finally fallen into Helmut's way of thinking, that it's better to leave the past *in* the past? Maybe I just needed breathing space to prepare me for what was to come.

Curiosity finally got the better of me after another week, and I decided to drop into the shop on my way home from uni to ask if they'd managed to transfer the film on to DVD. I zipped up my jacket as I left the lecture hall. The air felt crisp and earthy, with a distinct smell of smoky bonfires. The autumn sky was just one large grey flannel, but the trees on either side of the road were skirted by pools of gold and rust-coloured leaves. As the wind tore through them, they took to the air in a merry dance, pirouetting around the trunks. Once the wind calmed, the dance ended and the leaves came to rest in the same place as before.

'We've managed to save most of the sixteen millimetre film,' the shop assistant said, handing over the DVD. 'Not such good news about the old film roll, I'm afraid. It must have got wet at some stage, probably condensation. We were only able to salvage a few photos from the inner layer. It's the best we could do. The film is over sixty years old, after all,' he added apologetically.

Thanking him, I swept both items into my rucksack and rushed home. For the first time in my life I would be able to watch live pictures of my father as a young man and see the war through his eyes. I switched on my TV and DVD player and grabbed the remote control.

Just as I settled into my armchair with pen and notebook, the phone rang.

'Jonas Berger?' a German-sounding voice asked. 'It's Mrs Werther – from Vivat Independent Living. We spoke a few weeks ago, when you returned your mother's key. You were chatting with Frau Schuhmacher. Do you remember asking me for a copy of the book, and names of others in the writing group?'

'Yes, course I do. You've got some news?'

'Well, you'll be pleased to know that I found two more members, who still live here. They both have a copy of *Days of Fear*, and have fond memories of your mother. They said they'd be happy to talk to you.'

'Thanks for letting me know. That's really kind. I'll be coming over again in November, during reading week.

May I give you a ring nearer the time to arrange a visit?'

'Certainly. Their names are Mrs Rau and Mr Felz. I'll let them know.'

The book had finally surfaced. I'd be able to interview two more eyewitnesses about the war's final days. Brilliant.

Back to the DVD – labelled *1939–42*. Lives gone, traces left. Play. The opening screen says *Kodak 1939*. Wow, I didn't expect full colour. Pity there's no soundtrack. At the end of a long paved driveway is my grandparents' house. It's a large detached property – I guess five or six bedrooms – with a flat roof porch over the front door. An arched gateway to the right leads to a huge garden and a single-storey extension. The camera pans round in a circular movement to capture front and back gardens, both of which are surrounded by high mesh fences secured with concrete posts. A few sloping steps at the back of the house guide us to a small terraced garden with a gravelled seating area and an immaculately shaved lawn below, enclosed by neatly trimmed campanula. The garden is awash with shrubs, trees and roses. The tulips are beginning to bloom and the fruit trees coming into blossom.

The camera pans left to the patio. Grandad and Grandma come into view – people I recognise but never got to meet, as they died shortly after I was born. They are sitting at a table outside, studying a map – of Germany? Her friendly, round face smiles into the lens. She's wearing a flowery short-sleeved dress, and her white wavy hair is combed back from her forehead. When the camera zooms in on her face, she gestures to the cameraman to go away, grabs a book and settles down on a bench nearby.

Grandad rises slowly from his chair and follows her. He's a short, rotund, bespectacled man in a grey waistcoat over a white shirt and tie. His baggy trousers have slipped a bit, revealing a pair of braces that stop them falling down entirely. His crew cut seems to have gone wrong at the sides, which look bare and clean-shaven, leaving just a few streaks of brown thinning hair on top. His hands are covered with age spots, now visible in what must have been one of the first colour films. He's pointing to an empty flowerbed – room for more roses? When he lights his cigar, I recognise a signet ring on his left hand, the one he passed down to Dad. The ring that Helmut rejected before Dad died – in my view, a pointless act of defiance. It's engraved with Grandad's initials, *KFB* – Karl Ferdinand Berger. I still wear it, on and off. Grandad doubles back, walks over to the table and picks up a newspaper.

I wondered what news he would be reading. Maybe he was digesting the paper's right-wing propaganda about the Polish Corridor, which, as a result of the Versailles Treaty, gave Poland access to the Baltic Sea and thus divided Germany from its territory in East Prussia.

It's spring 1939. Poland is still safe, but the secret Hitler–Stalin Non-Aggression Pact will be signed in the summer, containing an additional clause to carve Poland up between them. Later in August, Hitler will introduce food rationing cards and petrol vouchers, and soon after the invasion in the autumn Adolf Eichmann will start deporting Jews from Austria and Czechoslovakia into Polish concentration camps. These won't be mentioned in any of the newspapers, however.

Would this have been the last spring my grandparents

enjoyed as a whole family? Still happy times? Did they have the slightest inkling of what was about to unfold?

Cut. Another opening screen appears: *Agfa 1939*. Grandad and Friedhelm, Dad's brother, bare-chested in the garden. It's clearly a hot summer's day. Suddenly Dad walks into the picture, a mere twenty-one, wearing black swimming trunks pulled right up over his navel. He falls to the ground, pretending to dive for cover, then aims his make-believe gun towards the camera. Both brothers look toned and fit after two years of military service. They perform 'burpees' – physical exercises – to impress their dad. They start in a standing position, drop into a squat with their hands on the ground, kick their feet back into a plank position, while keeping arms extended, then immediately return to the squat position and jump up. Grandad nods approvingly and comments. I imagine him saying something like 'You've turned out alright, after all. Remember: you're the future of Germany.'

Wipe. I'm surprised that in 1939 they had this optical effect, in which an image appears to 'wipe off' or push aside the preceding one. The next scene homes in on Dad; he fools around, impersonating Charlie Chaplin, his stiff body swaying from side to side, feet resting firmly on the ground. He turns an imaginary walking stick in his hand. Now he imitates Chaplin's walk, feet pointing outwards. He grins and repeats the same slapstick scene all over again, this time using a real walking stick.

Wipe. He walks over to his mother, who is lying on a deckchair, and rolls a heavy medicine ball down her body, which she appears to take in good spirits. Then the garden hose comes out and is attached to a sprinkler; mother and sons jump through the water jet to cool down. The scene ends with more physical games: the brothers hurl the medicine ball backwards and forwards, trying to knock each other off their feet. The parents join the fitness training, turning it into a calmer, less aggressive game.

Cut. We are still in 1939, but strangely enough it is no longer in colour. The first leaves have dropped on to the neatly manicured lawn. It's almost autumn. There will be war soon. My grandparents are locking the gate. A tiny dachshund follows them timidly as they go inside the house. Who is filming now? The camera pans left to a smaller, one-storey house that is part of the estate. It's an unassuming, whitewashed house with small windows and a narrow gable.

I pressed the Pause button.

Goodness! I recognised this house, since it appeared in a photo in my childhood album. I jumped up and grabbed the album from the shelf, quickly finding the photo of me, a two-year-old toddler, sitting naked under the cherry tree in front of the house in which I was born. I couldn't help smiling at the 'yummy' expression on my face, both hands clutching my protruding tummy, which looked as if it was full of cherries.

This was definitely my birthplace. The family GP delivered me at home – quite unusual at the time – and for years Helmut sowed seeds of doubt in my mind as to whether or not my mother and our doctor had been lovers. 'You could be his, 'cause you don't really look like you're my brother,' he used to tease me. Should I have been concerned?

I leaned back in my armchair and closed my eyes for a couple of minutes. Could Mother possibly have had an affair? I doubt it very much. You cannot choose your parents, nor the place you were born. It happens just by chance. I might not have been born in Germany at all. I might have been an American boy or perhaps even an English one. What would *that* have been like? To grow up in a country that won the war. I often wondered, if he had come here on holiday, what a solitary English boy would have made of occupied Germany after the war. Playing with me in the rubble probably wouldn't have been his idea of fun. And, besides, his parents wouldn't have sent him to this place for a holiday, a ruined country steeped in guilt and ugly memories, a country which for six long years their side had fought against in a bitter war. Would he have gloated, or cast accusations at me?

It sounds silly, but there was a character in my English textbook at grammar school called George, about my age. He became a lifelong imaginary friend, to the extent that I would have whole conversations with him – in private, of course. We became friends, gradually. We would talk about everything and anything: football, toys, even girls. His German was limited to a few words he'd picked up from English war films – *Achtung, Hände hoch, kaputt* – none of which seemed particularly useful for our conversation. We did argue occasionally, when we talked about the war, in particular if George reeled off disconcerting stats he'd heard in his history lessons.

'My parents lived in London during the war, you know. Our teacher said that 13,000 people were killed in the Blitz by German bombs.'

'I know, that's terrible, but does that justify the English raid on Dresden in 1945, where 500,000 civilians lost their lives? The war had already been won by that time.'

'Yes, but you started the war, you wanted total war.' He glared at me with an air of accusation.

'I wasn't even born then.' I tried to defend myself, but in the end there was no point; there was no justifiable defence. It all boiled down to the one question that George would never have to ask himself. And what did *your* parents do in the war?

I sat up, grabbed the remote and released the Pause button. Reverse angle shot from 'my house'. The majestic iron gate opens again, and Grandad's Opel Kapitän glides on to the premises. It's a convertible four-door saloon, and its radiator grille resembles a piece of protective armour, with two bulging headlights squeezed in between huge, puffed-up mudguards.

I stopped the film again and Googled the car. I found out that the Opel Kapitän was an executive car made by German car manufacturer Opel (now General Motors) between 1938 and 1970. Interesting. Not many people would have been able to afford a brand-new vehicle like that, so Grandad must have been doing very well before the war. I'd been told that he owned two machine tool factories, and when he lost everything in the war he still had to pay off his creditors, so everything came under the hammer. I remember Dad taking me along to buy back some of his parents' expensive furniture.

Medium-long shot. We are back in colour. The Opel Kapitän stops in front of the house. Two soldiers in

Wehrmacht uniform step out. It's only when the camera zooms in that I recognise the two brothers. There's a brief close-up of Dad's profile: straight nose, piercing blue eyes with neat dark eyebrows. Had they come back to say their last goodbyes? There's a sense of foreboding in this scene. Were they about to leave for the Front? All I know is that Dad wasn't involved in the invasion of Poland. I felt guilty watching these pictures of my uniformed father and uncle, as if I were somehow complicit, looking on the future face of horror. The horror that hadn't yet happened. Previously, I'd only seen pictures of German soldiers in English war films and had no idea what the different insignia symbolised. For example, the cockade surrounded by an oak leaf wreath on their *Schirmmütze*, the peaked cap with wire stiffener, and there was also the *Wehrmachtsadler*, the eagle worn above the right breast pocket. Seeing the brothers in full uniform – officers' hats, broad belt around their waists and long black leather boots – made me feel extremely uncomfortable. I pressed Pause.

I needed a break, so went into the kitchen to pour myself a large glass of red wine. It's like being in a different world, out there, I thought. Almost feels like Groundhog Day: you know what's going to happen next, but there's nothing you can do about it.

Play. The brothers in uniform – they are sitting on the garden wall puffing away at the last part of a cigarette held between thumb and index finger. When they stand up, I gather from Dad's vivid gestures that he's telling Friedhelm about the shooting down of an enemy plane. His extended arms imitate the flight path of the attacking plane, then his hands make a tumbling movement to suggest that the plane has taken a hit and crashes to the ground. He offers another cigarette from a silver case and they light up again. I notice from the different collar on Dad's uniform that he must be a higher-ranking officer than his brother, but I'm not exactly sure what the collar stripes signify. *One up on your younger brother, Herr Leutnant!*

Wipe. We are still in the garden. The brothers are no longer in uniform. Another fitness training scene – however, this time less playful and more daring. They are practising somersaults and backward flips on the lawn with an old mattress as a safety net. They don't always land on their feet. Then they put on their boxing gloves and fight as sparring partners in a friendly boxing game.

Cut. It looks like early autumn. The brothers are smartly dressed, in white shirt and tie, lying on wooden deckchairs. They start playfully pulling each other's tie and eventually wrestle each other off the chairs, which inevitably collapse underneath them. More play fighting follows on the lawn, simulating hand-to-hand combat, until they both fall to the ground and pretend to be dead. The screen turns black for a few seconds.

Cut. *Agfa 1940* appears on the screen. Pause.

I got up and paced nervously up and down the living room. Then went into the kitchen and poured myself another glass of red. Brief mental recap. This was the year when the German invasion turned to Northern and Western Europe at a frightening pace. Norway, Denmark, the Benelux countries and France all surrendered by the end of June. The Battle of Britain began in July and RAF

Bomber Command ordered night raids on Germany. The London Blitz followed in September. It started with Black Saturday on 7 September, the bombing of East London's docks. Night after night, waves of German bombers attacked British cities, ports and industrial areas. More and more countries joined the war. Italy, Japan, Slovakia, Hungary and Romania, all joined the Axis powers.

I put my glass down on the coffee table, grabbed the remote and pressed Play. Dad and brother Friedhelm arrive by car at their parents' home. They are on short-term leave. It looks like the middle of summer and France has already fallen. They greet their mum with a kiss and a hearty embrace. Grandad looks the other way and, clearly embarrassed, sticks another cigar in his mouth. He holds up a bottle of Champagne. Happy smiles all round. Time to celebrate …

Wipe. Another rapid transition. Dad's walking around the garden, playing the accordion – is this something he's picked up in Paris? Then there's a rare shot inside the house. The brothers are sitting at the breakfast table in the kitchen, both still in their bathrobes. Dad's reading the newspaper with the pet dachshund on his knee. When the camera zooms in, I can just about make out a front-page photo of German soldiers posing under the Arc de Triomphe sporting unbearably smug grins. The dog on Dad's lap gets restless and begins to wriggle. He raises his index finger and makes it stand on its hind legs. The dog obeys his orders. Grandmother comes in bringing a platter of cold meats, eggs and toast. Food rationing doesn't seem to have affected the Berger family – at least, not yet. For them, life continues as normal, untroubled by war. The screen turns black.

When it lights up again with an upside-down Agfa sign, we've skipped a year, moving on to the last section of the DVD. Apparently no footage survived of 1941. From my notes – the only time Dad told me where he'd been in the war – I can ascertain that he spent a whole year in Crete with the Wehrmacht Signal Corps, before moving on to Yugoslavia and mainland Greece. According to him, there was little resistance after the massive airborne invasion of Crete. However, the history books tell a different story: in retaliation to frequent attacks from partisans, German paratroopers carried out various massacres of male civilians, amongst them the infamous massacre in the olive groves of Kandomari. *You were there, Dad. Did you not know about it? Could you not tell me because you were ashamed, or even involved in some way?*

Play. 1942. There is no sign of the brothers. The iron gates are shut. Grandad opens the larger gate to the waiting car. He's wearing a smart suit, obviously dressed for a special occasion. The car, an even more luxurious model than Grandad's, stops close to the house. Guests wearing broad-rimmed hats and fur coats step out gingerly and wave to the camera like nobility. The men greet each other with pumping handshakes and light their cigars. A maid in a white apron takes the guests' presents and flowers. Have they come to do business with Grandad or is it just a social visit – maybe a birthday celebration? Soon afterwards another couple arrives, also in their mid-fifties. All of the guests are shown round the gardens. Grandad struts through the alcove like a military man. The guests line up for a group photo. He's taking a few snaps with what looks like an old Voigtländer camera. The flash goes off, leaving a small puff of smoke. Grandad checks his watch. Is it time for lunch? He frowns and shakes his wrist, then takes his watch off and rewinds it. No good. He shakes his head; the expensive-looking watch seems to have stopped. It's summer 1942. The carpet-bombing of Cologne by the Western Allies had started in May. The German advance into the Soviet Union would soon be halted and the battle of Stalingrad disastrously lost, a major turning of the tide of war in favour of the Allies. Ironically, the picture on this last bit of film turns fuzzy and stops abruptly.

I switched off the DVD player and TV. An intriguing record of seemingly ordinary lives in extraordinary times. In front of me on the coffee table lay my open notebook and pencil. I realised that I hadn't made a single note.

Chapter 6

In the first week of the new term, I'd taught my students how to work with primary sources. We'd studied and interpreted original documents, diaries, recordings, and other information sources created during the post-war period.

'Primary sources are the historian's raw materials. We must read and interpret them in a different way to history textbooks. These we call secondary sources, because they are interpretations of events created without first-hand experience,' I used to lecture them. 'We look at primary sources in their social and historical context, so we can make inferences that help us to understand what was going on at the time.'

On one occasion I had given them a facsimile of the Stalin Note, a document delivered in 1952 to the representatives of the Western Allies in which he presented the terms for German unification. 'How serious was Stalin's offer, and how was the Note perceived by the Allies? Look at Frank Roberts' handwritten notes in the margins. A wasted opportunity for early unification of Germany?' Discuss.

What would I be able to infer from *my* primary sources – Dad's film clips – in the context of the early war years between 1939 and 1942? There was one obvious conclusion: I come from a wealthy family on Dad's side. Grandad earned himself a small fortune with his machine tool factories, and was no doubt contributing to the war effort big time. Up to 1942, the whole family seemed unaffected by the war and led a comfortable life. However, there was no footage outside the parental home and the answer to my question remained a secret.

What did you do in the war, Dad? Yes, you looked comfortable and carefree at home in your officer's uniform, and judging by the story you told your brother about the shooting down of an enemy plane, I sense a certain degree of enthusiasm for the way the war was going. Most people shared your feelings. What were you thinking when you went to war? Did you think you were fighting for your country? For a just cause? And some time later, when you started having doubts, I assume you just fought on to save your comrades. But what happened when there was no one left at the end – when you were on your own? Back then, in 1940, you were treated as heroes. When you finally made it home at the end of the war, you were either a deserter or a war criminal, or even both.

'Most of this is mere speculation, sir. You can't make inferences from a silent movie where there's no war footage,' my students, quite rightly, would have objected. OK, let's return to the evidence. What other primary sources did I have? Well, of course there was Mum's war diary. Against all the odds I hoped we'd be able to retrieve it from somewhere, but it could be anywhere – if, indeed, it still existed. No doubt she would have written more about Dad and his whereabouts. All I had seen was a single diary page of 20 March 1945, where she'd described her flight from the Russians with her newborn baby. I wondered why she had kept hold of just this one page while the rest was missing. At least there were some German eyewitnesses I would be able to talk to. And then there was Mum's friend,

Elsa Kohl, now living somewhere in London. She'd be my best hope of finding the diary.

Saturday morning. I rang Mrs Werther at Vivat Independent Living to arrange an appointment with Mrs Rau and Mr Felz, the two remaining eyewitnesses. Perhaps they'd still be in touch with Elsa and might have her address. And, of course, I would see Mum and attempt to gently prompt her memory about the diary. I booked my flight for the second week in November – reading week.

More primary sources were stashed away in my rucksack, which still sat unopened on the hall floor. 'We were only able to salvage a few photos from the 35mm film,' the shop assistant had apologised profusely. But I had no appetite for more primary sources. I'd spent most of Friday afternoon viewing and re-viewing Dad's ciné film clips and felt mentally exhausted. It was as if I'd been cast out far into deep waters, to drift and swim as best I could among strong currents. The urge for closure about my parents' past had led me to loop back to a time where I thought I'd find answers to my vital questions. It felt more and more like a trial – *j'accuse*. May I present the next exhibit, your honour – photos taken by the accused in 1944.

Incriminating evidence of what, though? What could a few photos prove? If Dad had known there'd been anything untoward, he would surely have destroyed the film roll. Should I have thrown it in the bin, just in case, rather than have it developed in some strange laboratory? For a split second I was back in Dad's darkroom, submerging a piece of photographic paper into the developer bath, gently moving it around with a pair of tongs until the positive image miraculously appeared. It had been fun back then in his darkroom.

I don't know why I hadn't taken the photos out of their wallet in the photographer's to have a peek. Of course I was curious, strangely inquisitive, but I also felt some slight trepidation. I recalled Dad's stern voice telling me off as a youngster, when I'd nose around in other people's snaps while sorting out customers' orders. Would the shop assistant have done the same?

'But that's brilliant! More authentic sources to scrutinise and a few more eyewitnesses to interview,' Sam enthused when we clinked glasses in the Duke of Wellington. 'Cheers!' Then he added what sounded like a prudent health warning: 'Keep digging, but be prepared to find nasty surprises.' I didn't tell him that I hadn't looked at the photos yet.

Sam is co-writing our book *Fractured Lives*. He's also my friend and History department colleague. He's about my age, black hair greying at the sides. His rimless glasses sit between unruly eyebrows and a neatly trimmed beard. He hardly ever wears his Kippa in public. Sam had spent a long time researching his own family history in the Wiener Library for the Study of the Holocaust and Genocide, and had only recently discovered that his grandparents were murdered by the Nazis in 1941 in Izbica, one of the lesser-known Jewish ghettos in occupied Poland. Two years earlier, his dad had been rescued by the Kindertransport. I always thought Sam endured the excruciating pain of his family history with great stoicism. However, I didn't share his excitement for my additional authentic sources, fearing what else they might reveal. So far my sources didn't provide closure. And they now reminded me poignantly that, at the time when Dad was playing the fool, impersonating Charlie Chaplin and prancing around in his National Socialist uniform, Sam's father was living in constant fear of deportation.

I got up to get another round. The bartender, a young guy with pierced ears and a dragon tattoo on his arm, filled two pint glasses until they overflowed, spilling some of the ale on the counter. Would the bittersweet air of beer and cider, spilled on tables and floors night after night, linger here for ever? A bit of the past that will never change? Unlike family history, in its various permutations, which seems to reinvent itself with each new generation. As we got carried away discussing the eyewitness accounts we wanted to include in the book, all the smells seemed to dissipate. The nose forgot the fresh evening air outside, the eyes became accustomed to darkness and dimmed lights, and the ears were filled with the buzz of endless pub chatter. I shifted uneasily in my chair and felt my body fidgeting with small, jerky movements, like a fish trying to wriggle off the hook.

'What if I find something bad among Dad's photos? Something that will make me feel ashamed to be his son?'

'So you haven't even looked at them? Why not?'

'I don't know, I just felt—'

'Look, no one can choose their parents, and collective guilt shouldn't really apply to the post-war generation, don't you think? Remember Helmut Kohl's phrase – that our generation is "blessed by a later birth"? If it makes you feel any better, we can have a look at them together.'

'Really? What if—?'

'Do you think anything can shock me more than the pictures from the ghetto where my grandparents died?' He paused for a moment, took a handkerchief out of his pocket and blew his nose loudly, trying to distract attention from his breaking voice. 'The worst thing is, up to 1941 they still had a chance to leave Nazi Germany.' Tears started to well up.

'Why did they refuse to go?'

'Because Grandad was convinced that nothing would happen to him. He was a highly decorated First World War pilot. I still have a photo of him sitting in a double-decker plane sporting his iron cross. He felt German through and through. "*Mir wird schon nichts passieren.*" I'm sure nothing will happen to me. Dad remembers his words to this day.'

We sat in silence for a few minutes, staring at our half-empty glasses.

'Proud to be a German Jew. Sounds like a contradiction in terms, doesn't it?'

'Indeed,' Sam replied with a half-smile, shaking his head.

We drank up and agreed to pore over the photos in my office on Monday over lunch, searching for clues about my dad's wartime involvement.

'You may want to take another look at your parents' documents dated 1944 to 1945,' Sam said as we parted. 'There might be some vital connections that will help us to make sense of the photos.'

I felt strangely relieved. Maybe the university

environment would lend the viewing an air of official research. I would prepare a storyboard, label the photos with as much information as I could deduce and stick them on a piece of cardboard.

I opened my rucksack on Sunday morning with some trepidation. The sealed photo wallet felt thinner than expected. Four black-and-white photographs slipped out as I clumsily broke the seal. What I found was bizarre and profoundly shocking.

The first, a truly ghoulish picture, needed little explanation. It showed an execution scene. Around twenty hostages, at least one woman amongst them, were all dead or dying. They had been lined up against a crumbling brick wall on a narrow cobblestoned road. The officer seemed to be engaging in some finishing-off shots. In the background, in the shadow of some large chestnut oaks, German soldiers were witness to the horrific scene, hiding sheepishly under the trees. A merciless slaughter of innocent civilians – probably some act of retribution.

Why on earth would anybody photograph such a horrific war crime? *You took this picture, Dad, of the slaughtered, the innocent. Who killed them? Your men? Did you give the order? Or were you just a Mitläufer, a bystander and conformist, who let things happen?* Would he have had flashbacks later on in his life in his photography studio. Each time he'd pressed the exposure button, did it cause those execution moments to appear in the reflection of his Rolleiflex camera?

At first sight, the second picture looked straightforward: three people posing in front of a wooden shack built on to some half-concealed archway. A tall young woman, probably around twenty, and with blonde plaits, is flanked by two officers. Both have their arms around her. She wears the Party badge on her left breast pocket, which bears the oakleaf wreath and swastika. The inscription in silver letters reads *NSDAP* (National Socialist Workers' Party). The officer on her left is my father, wearing the same uniform as in the ciné film. On her right stands an officer in a black SS uniform. He doesn't smile, but just stares into the camera with cold eyes. His etched, birdlike face and hunched shoulders gave me the creeps. Around the trio, on the untidy patch of grass, a few daffodils are poking their heads through. If the writing on the original film roll is to be believed, the photos had been taken in 1944. That's as far as my forensic evidence goes. How could I find out who the other two people were? What was their relationship? And where was the photo taken? Perhaps Mother would be able to shed some light.

Next photo. It's winter. At the end of a churned-up muddy road, framed on either side by pollarded poplars, lie two unrecognisable dead soldiers near a destroyed tank. Only by Googling various tank models was I able to verify its Russian origin. Looking at this apocalyptic picture, I imagined the last minutes before the guns fell silent, when the tank drivers were mown down by German machine-gun fire as they deserted their tank, with their hands up.

Is this one of your last trophy pictures? Capturing the moment when German troops managed to halt the Soviet advance for a short while? I'm fairly sure that this photo was taken in western Poland, probably in January or February. I know from Mum's last letter to you that you were stationed near Liegnitz (now Legnica) from 1944 until spring 1945.

I got up from my desk to check a document that would corroborate the exact date. I had recently come across my parents' will in a box file containing various official documents – including their marriage certificate. I'd spotted the name Liegnitz on the will, on which I also found the date I was looking for: *Liegnitz, den 20. September 1944.* They'd made their will two months after the wedding, leaving their joint savings of 25,000 Reichsmark to the surviving partner. They must have thought the end was near and their chances of survival slim.

I went over to the bookshelf and re-read the chapter 'Digging in' from Nicholas Stargardt's *The German War*, one of the few books that explore diaries, letters and eyewitness accounts. In this particular chapter he describes the Soviet advance from September 1944. The tide of war was turning decisively against Germany and the troops faced defeat after defeat, retreat after retreat. For the captured German officer, the choice was stark: either swallow his cyanide capsule or become a prisoner of war, a fate that (in many cases) was probably worse. Millions of German civilians were now refugees fleeing westwards. Tens of thousands would not survive the arduous trek in the freezing winter.

The last photo was a selfie of Dad on his own, but he's hardly recognisable. He looks rough and utterly exhausted. He's shed his uniform and is disguised as a French prisoner of war, wearing a beret, a tricolour ribbon is buttonholed in a shabby grey jacket, and he's sporting a moustache. He's swapped his long leather boots for a pair of walking boots, which are falling apart at the seams. The blood-soaked bandage on his left thigh is coming apart, too. Grim-faced but determined to survive, he rests on a bench next to a signpost that says *Senftenberg*.

I'd never heard of this place, so I looked it up on Google Maps. It's a small town, around fifty kilometres north of Dresden, and, what's more interesting, 185 kilometres west of his last posting in Liegnitz. My head was spinning, desperately trying to make connections. Mother's letter from Ernsthausen, written in March 1945, must have reached him on the Eastern Front. Thus he would have known that his wife and his son had safely reached the West. What did we know about Dad's escape? He'd never talked about it, but Mum had. She'd told us they were reunited in Ernsthausen, in Hessen, on 30 May 1945. Apparently, he'd walked all the way back from the Front to Ernsthausen, around 500 kilometres, in just over three weeks – mainly at night, avoiding the main roads and towns. Also, the timescale – 8 May to 30 May 1945, three weeks from the end of the war – is about right. So this last photo proves that the film must have been in his camera from spring 1944 to May 1945. Just as well I shall never know the subject matter of the photos we'd been unable to recover. Would he have documented his arduous journey back home? According to Helmut, his odyssey had entered the family history as an 'heroic' event. Should I ring Helmut and tell him about my find? Maybe later.

I'd gripped each photo like the rung of a ladder by which I tried to haul myself closer to the action, back to my father's life. I tried to imagine what it had been like to live through this long stretch of war, day after day, year after year, not knowing when and how it would end.

Brief history recap:

By the end of the war the Eastern Front had descended into barbarity. Against the overwhelming Red Army forces, German troops were ordered to hold the line at any cost. They had no choice but to fight for their lives. Anyone found deserting, or stragglers suspected of doing so, would have faced the firing squad. German troops in Breslau (now Wrocław), about eighty kilometres east of Liegnitz, were besieged by Soviet forces, which had encircled the city as part of the Lower Silesian Offensive Operation. The German surrender on 6 May was followed by the surrender of all German forces two days after the battle.

Would Dad have told his troops to hold out until the end? Would he have yelled, 'The Führer gives us our orders, we will obey'? Or would he have released his men from their service oath following Hitler's death on 30 April 1945, telling them to get home as best they could? I think the latter is more likely. Did any of them survive? The only thing I can say for certain is that Dad made a superhuman effort to avoid capture, and managed to return safely to his wife and newborn son.

In the kitchen, I made myself a strong black coffee and raided the biscuit tin. Clasping the mug with both hands, I stood at the patio door and stared into the garden. The lawn was covered in dead leaves, obscuring what lay underneath.

By looking at these photos, how did Dad's world reveal itself to me? Was I making the right connections? Did the reconstructed fragments make sense? I wanted to understand his war involvement and how the experience had changed him. Helmut had told me as a child that Dad wasn't at the Front. As the war intensified, though, most soldiers would have taken part in state-sanctioned killings or face-to-face combat. I know very little about his part in the war crimes. He may not have committed any himself, but was in a position of authority as an officer, so may well have given orders to kill – and that is a crime. I now have some circumstantial evidence that makes me think he was involved in some killings.

Imagine what it must be like to grow up as a child of a mass murderer. It has to be the most terrible burden, living with that knowledge. Consider being the son of Hans Frank, Governor General of occupied Poland, responsible for all the Polish camps.

It doesn't matter who made them walk to the end of the plank and put the bullet in their heads. It doesn't matter who physically dropped the capsules through the vents in the gas chamber ceilings. The moral responsibility lay with the commanding officer. It's called command responsibility. *Were you fully committed, Dad, or just a cog in the system?*

I stuck the photos on a sheet of A4 cardboard, then labelled them up in chronological order, adding a caption, place and date:

1. *Dead soldiers near Russian tank – Poland – January/ February 1944*
2. *Dad with two unknown persons – near Liegnitz – spring 1944*
3. *Execution of civilians (Polish partisans?) – place unknown – summer 1944*

Even though Mum might be able to fill in some of the gaps – identify unknown people and places – there was always the danger that taking her back to the past would upset her, even endanger her life again, as it had during my last visit.

I lay awake for hours that night, tossing and turning. Eventually the tormenting thoughts of killings and executions faded. I closed my eyes, felt my limbs relax and almost reached the state where you feel safety in sleep. But then, at the brink of sleep, my father's starved face and open wound jolted me back into wakefulness. Lying on my back staring at the ceiling, I turned over in my mind the same tormenting thoughts and images. Then I'm with him on his journey back home, racking my brain as to how he managed to get food and drink, where he slept … how he coped with the constant fear of being arrested or killed.

'Take your pick. I've bought us some sandwiches,' Sam said with a smile as he came into my office on Monday. He dropped a selection on my desk, then went straight over to the pinboard.

'I see you've done your homework.' He was immediately drawn to the execution photo. Was he looking for the yellow armbands? Luckily, there were none.

'I'll never understand why my father took this gruesome photo.'

'I agree. It is rather strange, because members of the

Wehrmacht weren't allowed to take photos of executions, you know. The officer in charge must have asked him to take it, for whatever reason.'

In the silence that followed, Sam looked intently at the faded snapshot of Dad and the two unknown people, as though it were some mysterious hieroglyph that, if interpreted, might provide a clue, solve an enigma. Then he turned around to face me, biting his lower lip. Was he waiting for me to comment, or to make excuses? His initial smile, the one he'd used to greet me, had vanished. His face grew apprehensive; he leaned forward and took his hands out of his pockets.

'This is the clue, in case you're still wondering about the location,' he said matter-of-factly, his index finger hovering over the minute letters above the archway. It said *frei*. It didn't take much imagination to reconstruct the beginning of the slogan *'Arbeit macht frei'* – 'Work sets you free' – that appeared on so many concentration camp gates. I gazed into his face, so familiar and now so strange, like the face of an accuser, white and motionless. For a second his head turned into a skull. My heart pounded harder and harder. I felt his complete inability to afford me the least comfort.

'As historians, we should see these things through the eyes of a detached observer,' Sam said coldly. 'All it proves is that your dad knew of the existence of concentration camps. Let's not pretend: most ordinary Germans knew about the terror of Hitler's Holocaust – they knew what happened in the camps.'

'But why would you want to be photographed in front of … I don't understand … And I've no idea who this

74

woman and the SS man are.'

'She could be a friend, or a lover of either of them, or perhaps a prison guard? But she's definitely a proud Party member, wearing a badge with the swastika.'

He went back to my desk, rested his chin on his hand and stroked his beard pensively. 'Can I use your computer for a few moments?' he asked. 'If your dad was stationed near Liegnitz, we should be able to find out the name of the nearest camp.'

It took him just a few minutes to display a map headed *The Holocaust in occupied Poland*, which I'd never seen before. Like a pockmarked face, it recorded more than thirty different camps, identified by three different icons: skulls for extermination camps such as Treblinka, Chełmno, Majdanek and Auschwitz-Birkenau; the Star of David on a red background for major cities with ghettos; and a simple black square for the remaining concentration camps. Groß-Rosen in Lower Silesia, now called Rogoźnica, in present-day western Poland, was marked with a black square. We checked the distance from Liegnitz to Groß-Rosen: only twenty-nine kilometres.

I felt sick and excused myself. I needed some fresh air. The sky was hung with various shades of grey, then a fine rain started to fall. Since I didn't have any lectures in the afternoon, I wanted to walk home, feel the rain on my face. I wanted, needed, nature to cleanse me – body and soul.

Chapter 7

A few hours after I'd left the office – it was still early Monday afternoon – I rang Sam from home and apologised for leaving so abruptly. I couldn't face having lunch with him; couldn't face any more revelations. Sam's astute detective work, which uncovered where one of Dad's photos had been taken, the camp in Groß-Rosen, had made me recoil in horror. I just wanted to get stuck into my lecture preparation, as it would provide temporary respite from my family research.

My study looked messier than normal. Stacks of books everywhere – jumbled papers, Post-its, pencils and highlighters, all strewn across the desk – not to mention two stained coffee mugs next to my PC that hadn't been rinsed for days. On my bookrest, slightly at an angle, sat a copy of Mary Fulbrook's *German National Identity After the Holocaust*. Strangely enough, after taking some notes, I'd left it open on chapter 3, 'Overcoming the Past in Practice? Trials and Tribulations'. I hastily closed it and put it back on the jam-packed bookshelves that covered every spare centimetre of my study's walls. In the small gap by the window hung Edvard Munch's *The Scream*, which had fascinated me ever since I was a child. Perhaps it did so because I used to cover my ears when my parents argued, just like the distorted child on the bridge. I kept staring at the painting and, for the first time, noticed two shapeless black figures tucked away in the background at the end of the bridge. They looked like the walking dead – the child's parents? The screaming child is in agony, fearing being sucked into an inferno of flames and destruction.

Would a painter have portrayed Dad and me with outstretched arms – desperately, in vain, attempting to reach one other? Or would they have depicted us in a pose expressing relief, separated by a double barrier? Should we have been grateful for the protection that guarded us from each other's strangeness? What if we had confronted each other, unprotected by the rail of history? If nothing had stood between us any more, would we have tumbled into each other's arms?

Why this remoteness, Father; this reticence to speak out about your past? Why didn't you learn to talk about yourself and your feelings, to talk about those terrible memories? I will tell you why: it was too comfortable for you, it was so bloody comfortable for you, to hide in the darkroom of your photography shop, developing other people's pasts. Did it ever occur to you how much of a burden it was for us, not knowing but feeling your pain and humiliation, and seeing the wound on your leg that would never heal? Your mute, heroic endurance, probably not without vanity, caused more anguish for us than if you had shared some of those repressed memories. Even many years after the war, when the distressing images of unimaginable inhumanity were brought to public attention in the Frankfurt Auschwitz trials, you opted to stay silent and join the collective amnesia. If only you could have confided in us, Dad. It might have helped to strip away the omnipotence of your tormented past. Who knows: it may even have staunched your weeping wound. Isn't it part of human dignity to have the strength to acknowledge one's guilt, hard as that may be? I wonder whether I will be able to make peace with you now that I have acknowledged your obscure crimes, however bad they may have been.

In 1963, I was thirteen years old, and Grandma, the only one in our house who owned a television, wouldn't allow us to watch the Auschwitz trials. So, for us, the myth of collective innocence was still kept alive at that time: There were virtually no perpetrators; just a few war criminals who committed some awful crimes, and the victims had been restituted. End of story.

The truth was finally revealed to our generation in the late 1960s and 1970s. The first written account I can remember occurred in my A-level History textbook, in 1969. It summarised the Holocaust in just under 500 words, but devoted seven pages to the coverage of the Resistance movement, illustrated by large-scale photographs of Claus von Stauffenberg and Sophie and Hans Scholl. It didn't make us feel any better. Even more distressing, however, was the broadcast of *Holocaust*, the American mini-series, which, for the first time, brought the matter of genocide during the war to widespread public attention. Twenty million people watched the series in West Germany. After the broadcast, the historians' panel was overwhelmed by thousands of phone calls from shocked and outraged viewers.

We rebelled against our parents, teachers, civil servants, representatives of the state. Numerous former Nazi Party members were sitting in the German parliament. Even the Chancellor, Kurt Georg Kiesinger had joined the Nazi Party in 1933 as a young lawyer and worked in the Foreign Ministry's propaganda division during the war. Carl Carsten, parliament's president from 1976 to 1979, had been a member of the *Sturmabteilung* (SA) – the paramilitary wing of the Nazi Party – as we found out much later. He had been cleared by an Allied denazification court.

We condemned our parents' generation to shame, even if the only charge we could bring against them was that they had tolerated perpetrators in their midst. The more ghastly the events we read and heard about, the more certain we became of our responsibility to enlighten and accuse. Denazification in the western zones had been a farce, a matter of issuing *Persilscheine* ('Persil certificates'), to provide assurance of political cleansing so that people could return to their former positions in life. Like our Latin teacher, a former Luftwaffe pilot, who spent a great deal of his lessons talking about his 'heroic adventures' – the shooting down of enemy planes.

Actually, the youth protests of the late 1960s and 1970s form a major part in my lecture series for this term, which I will spice up with some of my own eyewitness accounts. I will explain, for example, how hard it had been for me to go through the process of being acknowledged as a conscientious objector, facing a tribunal of old Nazis. Any anti-military or pacifist tendencies were anathema to them. They tried to trick me – presenting hypothetical situations of self-defence, which they equated with a scenario in which Germany had to defend herself if attacked. Despite facing a prison sentence, I refused to do the mandatory military service. It was Helmut, rather than Dad, who had given me legal advice when I prepared and presented my case. We were united, then, in a common cause. Months later, I finally won my case in the appeal court. It was a case won on secular, not religious, moral principles. I have no memory of Dad putting his arm around my shoulder to say, 'Well done, lad.'

Back to my lecture preparation. What else, apart from Fulbrook's book needed to go on the reading list? Definitely Alexander and Margarete Mitscherlich's *The Inability to Mourn: Principles of Collective Behavior*. It was one of the first books I had read at uni, and asks why the Holocaust, the war crimes and the sentiment of guilt were not dealt with adequately in post-war German society. And, for the few students who could read books in German, I wanted to include Welzer et al.'s *Opa war kein Nazi*, which examines the ways stories and histories of National Socialism and the Holocaust are passed on from one generation to the next. These often end up as distorted or even embellished stories, exposing the sharp difference between official historic discourse and private memory. Why did this remind me of Helmut? I felt I should ring him and tell him about my new findings.

As predicted, he didn't share my sentiments about the discoveries. Neither the ciné film nor the photos seemed to interest him much. It was as if he'd already seen and dealt with some of these sources, and simply was not prepared to enter into any further discussion.

'Exploring the family past again, are we?' he said dismissively when I rang. 'You know, for me, the father chapter is closed once and for all.'

'Well, at least my colleague in the History department shares my interest in my family research.'

'Don't you think it's become a bit of an obsession? If I

were you, I'd leave things well alone. You're only giving us a bad name abroad. All of this happened a very long time ago.'

I changed the subject and asked about Mum. He said she'd almost fully recovered and was now back in her care home. I told Helmut that I'd booked my flight for the second week in November – reading week. I expected a 'Go easy on Mother' from him, but he just said, 'She'll be pleased to see you. I'll pick you up from the airport.'

I planned to spend one or two nights at Helmut's in Cologne. I would visit Mum the next day in her care home, then travel to her former Vivat home in Bad Iburg to meet with my new eyewitnesses, Mrs Rau and Mr Felz. I wanted to hear their stories from *Days of Fear*.

Rummaging through my shoebox of old photos, I wanted to find a few uncontroversial pictures of Mum's time in the BdM that would take her gently back to the past. Moments later I found her, leading a group of ten- to twelve-year-old girls on an excursion, marching in twos through the forest – a young woman, around eighteen, dressed like her girls in a white blouse over a long black skirt, sporting a black neckerchief and leather woggle. The standard-bearer, a blonde girl with plaits, carried the flag with the swastika and the words *Glauben und Rein Sein* ('Faith and Purity').

I would also show her the photo of the young woman in the BdM uniform posing with Dad and the SS officer and, of course, the one of Dad disguised as a French prisoner of war. What emotions, what memories, would these photos evoke? I had read that when we search the depths of our memory, we don't just reproduce the past, but we recreate it in our mind. I wanted to step back into her world in order to understand a part of our history, to see things through her eyes. By taking her back in time, I might also trigger her to remember what happened to her missing diary – or so I hoped.

A bitterly cold wind licked at my face and crept under my jacket as I stepped out of Cologne-Bonn airport, making my way to the outdoor car park where Helmut was waiting. A bear hug and a pat on the shoulder had become the standard ritual when we hadn't seen each other for a while. On our journey back, snow began to fall – unusual for mid-November. The flakes looked bright and sparkly against the grey sky. They fell on and on, effortless and unstoppable, trying to settle on the windscreen. They held their star shape for a split second before sliding hopelessly down the glass and being washed away by the wipers.

I considered all the daily impressions we're exposed to, hundreds of them like tiny snowflakes – many of them wiped away from our short-term memory in an instance, others getting compacted like snow, staying in our mind for a while, then gradually melting away. How does the world get into our heads and turn into memory? How do we decide what to keep and what to discard, and how do we get back to the past? Each time we unlock a memory, it seems to become unstable, in need of consolidation, before we put it back into our memory safe. But is it still the same? Do our eyewitness accounts provide us with a true picture of an historical event, or do they merely present one version of the truth?

Helmut had told me on the phone that 'The father chapter is closed.' But is it ever? Or did he just feel the need to protect himself from reopening a wound that had gradually healed? I could see my twelve-year old self standing frozen in the doorway, watching my Dad brutally hammering his fists on my brother's back for failing his end-of-term school exam. 'That's enough,' my mother eventually interfered and took the crying boy in her arms. I remembered Helmut swearing revenge on Dad afterwards. The memory of the beaten brother stayed in my head like the jagged pain of running your tongue over a broken tooth.

Life continued as before. But I shall never forget the look on his face when our eyes met as he cowered in the corner of the dining room: bereft, disillusioned. We both knew the father–son relationship had changed, that the trust and closeness had gone for ever. Maybe Helmut had erased this childhood event from his memory, or would he simply recount it differently to me? Perhaps, if put on the spot, he would even find excuses for Dad's behaviour: 'You know, Jonas, war brutalises people …'

'You're very quiet.' Helmut interrupted my thoughts as we took the exit from the motorway. 'How are things at home? Met anybody yet? Or are you just burying your head in your book?'

'No, I don't get out much these days. I know I should. And yes, I still have lots to do on the book. How's Mother?'

'She's blissfully happy. I think. I bought her some flowers the other day. A few minutes later, she asked me, "Who gave me these lovely flowers?"'

'Ah, poor Mum. At least she's happy in herself. She'll

be able to enjoy my Kinder chocolates several times over, then!'

He laughed briefly. Then the smile faded from his face, he sighed and shook his head. I noticed his grip tightening on the steering wheel.

'What I find rather disturbing, though, is that she has developed this strange fetish of searching for her diary. She keeps opening all her drawers, rifles through old papers and turns the whole place upside down. Not sure what *that's* all about.'

Something in his tone struck me. Had my inquisitiveness about her war diary caused this inner turmoil? I changed the subject. For the rest of the journey we exchanged pleasantries without revealing the true purpose of my visit. The snow had stopped falling as we arrived at his house, but heavy, grey clouds still loomed overhead.

In the evening we settled down to a generous *Abendbrot* – a variety of German dark breads, a cold meat platter, huge cheeseboard and a bottle of *Spätburgunder*. From time to time, Helmut got up to put another log onto the fire. There's something inviting about the look, familiar scent and warmth of a crackling wood-burning fire. We had a good old chat, reminiscing about our childhood. At one point we mimicked each other, starting each sentence with 'I used to ...' and burst out laughing.

I don't know what possessed me to destroy that relaxed and peaceful atmosphere. Maybe talking about us as children having to go on long Sunday walks with Mum and Dad was the trigger. I reached for my rucksack.

'By the way, can I show you just a couple of photos which were on the old film I found in my cigar box – you know, the one you gave me when we cleared out Mum's flat?'

He leaned back in his chair, arms folded across his chest, and took a deep breath. 'You just can't let go, can you?' he said, shaking his head. 'Alright, show me, if it makes you feel any better.'

I showed him the photo of the execution scene and the one Dad had taken of himself disguised as a Frenchman.

'I know. That's horrendous,' he said glancing at the first one. 'I came across a couple of similar ones before. I fished them out of the shoebox before you took it home with you. I shredded them, because I never ever wanted to see them again.'

'Is that all you have to say?'

'What do you mean?'

'Don't you understand? This is evidence of a war crime. Look, it's clear from the picture that they had already given themselves up. Some of them are lying there with their hands still up.'

'And what would *you* have done? Intervened and got shot yourself? What could Dad have done?' He paused for a moment to gather his thoughts. 'It's easy for us, in retrospect, to take the moral high ground. They were probably partisans who had shot German soldiers. It was war. War crimes happen. Look at the Iraq war. The Americans, the Brits, the Iraqis – they all committed horrible war crimes. That doesn't mean that I condone them, but that's what happens in wartime.'

'But why—?' He'd already picked up the other photo and stared at it for a long time without saying a word. It was clear from his reaction that he hadn't seen this one before. He appeared pensive and troubled. The inner corners of his eyebrows angled upwards and his eyelids drooped slightly. What was going through his mind? The expression on his face seemed to take him back to a sad memory. Silence.

'What?' I asked.

'You want more? Do you really want to hear what happened to him before he took the selfie?' he asked, a hint of disapproval in his voice.

'How do you mean?'

'In my job as a judge, not only do I listen to both sides of the story before I reach a conclusion, but I also engage with the whole case study. I need to know what happened before. And it's the same with these snapshots. They just capture a moment in time. You shouldn't interpret them without knowing the facts. What happened before he took these photos?'

'Well, we don't know,' I said, but it's not too difficult to deduce why he tried to disguise himself as a Frenchman.'

Helmut got up from his armchair and left the room. The wooden stairs made a distinctive creaky sound under his feet. What was all that about? I'd always had a nagging suspicion that he might know more about Dad than he was letting on. Would he come back with more snaps to show me what happened to Dad before he'd set the self-timer? It seemed unlikely that he'd have kept any more photos, given his reluctance to engage with family history. He returned a few minutes later, holding an envelope that had the yellow patina of old age.

'I could never decide when would be the right time to let you have this,' he said, handing it to me. 'You can keep it or throw it away. But I don't want it back.' His words sounded firm but calm.

Köln, September 1963
My dear son,
Over the past years I've started so many letters to you and thrown them all away. I thought you, and certainly Jonas, were too young to be burdened with some of the terrible things that happened to me in the war. But now that you are eighteen, I feel I can entrust you with an event that still haunts me to this day and may explain some of my (violent) mood swings, which I'm sure haven't gone unnoticed. Apologies – it's not how I used to be. One day, but not yet, you may wish to show this letter to Jonas. I leave it to you to decide when the time is right.

Until March 1944, my part in the war had mainly taken place over the phone. But then everything changed. Authorities, code-names, superior officers, changed every day. We joined a special contingent of 25 men and were deployed to the Eastern Front. There was a French POW and three fourteen-year-old kids amongst us. They thought that war was mainly about fighting. I told them they were wrong. It's about waiting. Waiting for the next attack, for the next meal, for the next morning. To wake up and think, 'God, you're still alive.'

This is the event I simply cannot erase from my mind: On 15 March 1945 we received orders from General Niehoff to move our small remaining contingent of

troops from Liegnitz to Breslau in Lower Silesia.
The aim was to clear a nearby airstrip so that the
Luftwaffe could supply the beleaguered city with food
and ammunition. As we approached the airstrip, we
spotted, at a distance, three low-flying Red Army
planes – the dreaded Ilyushin Il-2. I shouted, 'Take
cover,' and we all threw ourselves into the ditch by the
roadside, machine guns pointing up at the approaching
aircraft. The only thing I remembered after that was
the accelerating machine-gun fire on both sides, ending
with a loud bang. And suddenly there was silence. I
lifted my head out of the mud, and although I'd been
hit in the thigh, I managed to slowly pick myself up.
I shouted, 'Everybody fall in!' I was expecting them
to line up on the road. But nobody moved. When
the smoke lifted, I sank down on my knees and cried
– it was like Guernica burning. Maimed bodies
like slaughtered cattle scattered all over the ditches,
comrades in blood-soaked uniforms, limbs wrenched off
torsos. 'Fall in, for fuck's sake,' I screamed again and
again. Nothing. There were no survivors.

Why did I survive? I felt so guilty. Where were the
souls of my men who'd followed my lead and trudged
through the heavy snow with me? Some of them I had
known for years. They had laughed with me in 1942,
thinking we would soon eat caviar in Moscow when
we had only five hundred kilometres to cover. They were
comrades who'd become friends. Men who trusted me,
fought with me, drunk and shivered with me.

On my own, utterly bereft and exhausted, I dragged

myself into the nearby woods. I was safe for the
moment … As a medical student I had learned how
to disinfect and bandage my wound properly, but
there was no way I could get the shrapnel out. In
the evening I recovered the field telephone and rang
General Niehoff to debrief him and ask his men to bury
the dead. However, I didn't give him my real name, I
didn't want anyone to know I was still alive. For me,
the war was over.

'I have a son now,' I said to myself. Your mother wrote
to me that we have a son, Helmut, and that she was
fleeing with you to relatives in the West. That was the
last and best Feldpost I ever received. I just had to
believe that you would make it, that you were both still
alive. Clinging to that very thought is what gave me
the strength to survive against all odds. That's when
my odyssey began.

You've heard the rest of my story from Mum, who still
likes talking about my 'heroic' escape. I was anything
but a hero. A soldier for eight long years – and, at the
end, a broken man, deluded and destitute. I felt so
ashamed of myself. How will your generation ever be
able to understand what happened to us? How will you
judge us?

I hope I have the strength to give you this letter.

With all my love to both of you,
Dad

We sat for ages in an uneasy silence. My hand was still shaking as I put down the letter. Helmut passed me a tissue.

'I'm sorry. I didn't mean to—'

'No, it's quite alright. I always thought you knew things about him that I didn't. Even when we were children.' My voice was breaking up. 'Do you remember, you always told me he wasn't at the Front.'

Helmut came over, sat next to me and put his arm round my shoulder. 'And that was true for most of the time, until the end.'

'It's so sad. You were right: war changes people for good; it affects body and soul. I just wish we could have talked about it while he was still alive.'

'So do I. He never said, "I have to tell you something." He just handed me the letter and that was it. Never wanted to talk about it, never mentioned it again.'

'Just like you.'

'I'm sorry – I'm a rotten brother. I should have given you the letter a long time ago. I couldn't bear—'

'No, I understand. You formed your judgment and rested the case. But for me it's more than family history. It's like a giant piece of a jigsaw, with loads of different pieces that make up a story that needs to be told again and again to the next generation. They have to be able to see things from different perspectives so they can form their *own* opinion. That's why I'm gathering different bystander accounts while it is still possible. And that's what I'm trying to do in my book.'

'I know. I just hope you'll treat them with care and respect. Not everybody wants to be reminded of their past.

And just go easy on Mother tomorrow. You upset her quite a lot last time.'

Chapter 8

After breakfast, Helmut dropped me at Mum's care home on his way to the courthouse. Although the sky looked menacing, here and there a few rays of sunshine were nudging their way through the clouds. A cool breeze stirred and died, then again swelled into motion. A few elderly residents sat wrapped in blankets on their narrow balconies, their heads tilted back as though drinking in a new life from the autumn sun.

Searching for the print of August Macke's *Lady in Green Jacket* on the door, I found my way along the orange-coloured corridor to Mum's apartment. I knocked gently. No answer. Maybe she wasn't wearing her hearing aid, or was still asleep. I entered quietly, so as not to wake her, but she wasn't in her room. I left the flowers and my present – a Kinder chocolate advent calendar – on the table.

'Mrs Berger is in the common room,' said the nurse who'd spotted me in the corridor. 'She's gone to our weekly painting session. Come and have a look – you'll be amazed how good they are.'

As I stood at the threshold of the common room looking for Mum, an intoxicating mixture of oil paints and turpentine wafted towards me. A small group of elderly women sat slightly stooped in front of easels, brushes and freshly mixed palettes at the ready. They were painting a still-life – an oval-shaped terracotta vase containing a bunch of slightly limp sunflowers that had clearly seen better days.

'We're blocking in,' a lady wearing a body-warmer near to me explained expertly, as she brushed a flat layer of reddish-brown colour on to the canvas. Mum looked up at me and made eye contact. She nearly dropped her brush. I wended my way through easels and chairs to greet her.

'Jonas, what a lovely surprise!' She put down her palette, stood up and announced proudly: 'This is my son, who lives in England. He's come all this way to see his mother.'

Heads turned. All eyes on me. For a moment I felt they'd stopped painting a still-life and had decided to do a drawing of me. I quickly wiped from my mind the thought of having to pose for them in the nude ...

'Please don't let me interrupt your class, ladies.'

I turned to Mum. 'Just carry on for a while. We'll chat later.' Then, glancing at the nurse, I added, 'I'll be very quiet and just watch, if that's OK?'

Mum had already sketched the vase and three perfect-looking sunflowers in thin pencil lines. Moments later she was dabbing specks of yellow, brown and green oil paint on to the canvas. 'The sunflower is my favourite,' she said in a low voice, as though whispering to a classmate. 'They always show you the right way; turn their heads towards the sun, leaving the dark shadows behind.'

I remembered how as a child I'd loved picking the good seeds from the dried sunflower heads and discarding the bad ones. We'd store them in a small plastic container, and then plant them in spring, after the last frost. Mother liked the way that things were either right or wrong, light or dark, with no shades of grey in between. But there were lots of dark shadows in her life, and Dad's, and I was eager to shed some light on them.

I stood by her chair, admiring how steady her hand was on the canvas.

'That's very good, you know,' I whispered back.

'I only copy what I see – always have done. I'm not very good, really.' The lady in the body-warmer raised her eyebrows and shushed us. Everybody carried on painting in silence.

The sound of footsteps announced the end of the session. I looked up to see a nurse approaching with long energetic strides, then turning sharply into the common room.

'That's it for today, ladies. Well done, everybody. Let's all tidy up,' she announced clearly. 'Lunch will be ready in fifteen minutes.'

I helped to fold up the easels and returned them to the storeroom.

'I'm taking you out for lunch, Mum,' I said on my return.

'That's nice, but only if you let me pay.'

'We'll see. I'll just let the office know that we're going out. See you in your room in a minute.'

I took longer than anticipated. There was paperwork to do, as I needed to agree to her GP's change in medication.

'Where did you put the flowers and the advent calendar I brought you?'

'What? Oh, yes, someone left a bunch of flowers on my table, so I gave them back to the nurse.'

'But Mum, they were for you. I brought them for *you.*'

Then I spotted the advent calendar in the waste-paper basket – an empty shell with the back ripped off, all the chocolates missing.

'Mum, it's an advent calendar. You weren't supposed to eat all of the chocolates at once. One a day. It's not even December.'

'There were only a few left and I was hungry,' she said sheepishly with the guilty face of a child. 'Is Helmut coming to have supper with us?'

'No, Mum, he's at work. He'll come and see you on Saturday. *I'm* taking you out for lunch today.'

'Can you write it down for me? Or put it on my wall calendar, so I don't forget. Everything's so muddled these days.'

Poor Mum. She didn't know what time of day it was, let alone what day of the week or even which month. She no longer wore a watch – she'd squirrelled it away in her bedside drawer, where its futile hands turned round and round, ticking away into the void.

When I went to write on her calendar, I noticed that Helmut's visit had already been pencilled in. I also found repeated entries in Mum's handwriting saying, *Look for my diary*, and remembered Helmut's concern over her frantic searching.

Mum stretched out her hand. I took it firmly, to help her stand up. I turned her Zimmer frame round and guided it towards her. We were walking slowly down to the exit when she suddenly pulled the brake on the frame, turned towards me and said: 'How do you like it here?' And, without waiting for an answer, she added, 'You know, I would never want to live in an old people's home.' She was blissfully happy, just as Helmut had suggested on our way back from the airport.

Shortly before we reached the exit, we met a fellow

resident, who acknowledged us with a smile. And, without any introduction, she started to tell us her life story, cut short only by the polite intervention of her daughter.

'I don't know who *that* was. I didn't invite her into my house – what a cheek!' Mum said indignantly on the way out.

After a half-eaten lunch – Mum understandably didn't have much of an appetite – we chatted over coffee.

'Look what I found when we were clearing out your flat! Some ancient photographs in a shoebox.' My artificial-sounding enthusiasm wasn't exactly infectious. I showed her the Hitler Youth photo – Mum as an eighteen-year-old BdM leader.

'Look. That's you – and you look so pretty.'

She leaned forwards to take a closer look, trying to peer through narrowed eyes. Squinting didn't help. She rummaged through her handbag to find her glasses. As she took the photo in both hands, gazing at it intently, I searched her face for any sign of recognition.

'That's me,' she exclaimed, her body twitching with animation. A stifled laugh followed. 'That was an awfully long time ago …' She turned the picture over and read the faint pencil marks: *Breslau, 1941*. 'Goodness gracious! How old was I then?'

'It looks like you were leading a group of young girls on a hike through the forest.'

She tilted her head slightly in thought. As she used to do when dipping into her past, she began twisting her wedding ring around her finger to conjure up bygone images. 'We did have fun in those days …' She paused, searching the depths of her memory for happy events.

'Lots of excursions into the countryside,' I prompted.

She smiled. 'Yes, playing scavenger hunt in the forest, singing by the campfire … And once a week I organised a social evening. The girls loved the handicrafts workshop and choir practice. I was in charge of seventy-five girls, you know. As BdM leader, I had to attend weekly training sessions, where we learned new songs to pass on.'

'What else did they teach you?' I felt a bit like a memory hacker.

'Well, you know … They told us about plans for a greater Germany, we learned about the life of important party leaders, and we were informed about our enemies. But at the time I wasn't aware of any political indoctrination. There was no time to question things.'

The initial serenity faded from her face. Mother was no longer sitting upright, but slumped back in her chair, eyes lowered, fingers fiddling with the tassels of the old-fashioned tablecloth. She sighed, and her voice took on a worried edge.

'It would have been around that time that we received orders to evacuate children from areas at risk of bombing. They used to call it "housing action" rather than "evacuation". I got sent to a children's home near Breslau, in Lower Silesia, where I had to look after a large group of ten- to fourteen-year-old girls who'd never been away from home. Very different from our campsite and youth-hostelling days. Most of the girls didn't know each other, coming from places like Cologne, Düsseldorf and Essen. They were homesick, argued and cried a lot. It wasn't easy. I had just one teacher to help me organise their daily routines. It took us a whole week of just playing games and getting to know each other before we could resume normal lessons.'

In the silence that followed I did a quick mental fact check. I studied at Cologne University and knew its history well. The city was bombed in over 250 separate air raids by the Royal Air Force. The nightly carpet-bombing started in May 1940, and by 1942 the city was utterly devastated. However, amidst the ruins, the twin spires of the cathedral stood tall. They survived the bombing. Avoiding its destruction was not an act of mercy or respect for its cultural value – the British pilots had simply used the cathedral as a location reference point, to help them hit their targets more accurately. Just as in the London Blitz, both the Luftwaffe and RAF failed to deliver the intended knockout blow – destroying enemy morale.

I poured Mum another cup of coffee, got up and gently dabbed her weeping eye. She briefly held my hand in hers, and it felt warm and soft.

'You're OK? Look, I found another photo from that era. Dad's in this one as a young soldier. I have no idea who the other two people are.'

She sat up again and blew her nose. 'That must be … ' she began deliberately. But she wasn't sure of her ground, and the conversation came to an abrupt end.

'Who do you think it might be? A friend?'

'No, *that* man,' pointing to the SS officer. 'I don't know why she married him. He was a bad man.'

'Who married whom? Do you remember their names?'

'Yes. You know, that's my friend Elsa. She was my

subordinate in the BdM. She married him, Herbert Kohl. He was sentenced to death at the Nuremberg trials. I don't know why she married him. I never liked him.'

'And how did Dad know Elsa?'

'Elsa was sent to a children's evacuation camp near Liegnitz, where Rudi's contingent was stationed later in the war. The three of us met up occasionally – when circumstances allowed.'

My head was spinning with excitement. I did a brief recap, like I used to do for my students at the end of a lecture. Mum and Elsa Kohl had lived in the same Vivat home, and had been part of the creative writing group, working together on *Days of Fear*. But they'd also known each other before the war, as comrades in the BdM. Dad knew both Herbert and Elsa Kohl. But why was the photo taken in front of the notorious concentration camp?

I remembered that the writing group didn't like Elsa – possibly because her husband turned out to be a war criminal. They didn't mind losing contact with her when she moved to be with her niece in London. But was Mum still in touch with her? Did Elsa ever write to her? And, if Elsa had been Mum's close friend, it was possible she might know what happened to the war diary. I had to dig even deeper.

'Have you kept in touch with Elsa?' I asked innocently. 'You worked together on *Days of Fear*, didn't you?'

'Yes, we wrote about our experiences in the war, but her contribution was rejected by the editor. Bless her, she wasn't a very gifted writer. She often copied things from me and then changed the story a bit to make it her own. I think there were also some anti-Semitic passages in her piece, and that's probably why her story didn't get published.'

'Have you not seen her since you moved to your new home?'

'I don't remember. But all my things are still with her.'

'What do you mean? What things?' I was sitting on the edge of my chair.

'She looked after my things in the war. We were neighbours – she salvaged things when our flat was bombed out. Quite fearless, she was.'

'What sort of things?'

Mum ignored my question and made a move to stand up. 'I need the toilet. And then we must go back; it'll be getting dark soon.'

I helped her up and pushed the frame towards her. She gripped its handles and trundled off to the Ladies'.

I was worried how she might react if I pursued the salvage theme any further. I certainly didn't want to repeat the line of questioning that at my last visit had made her relive the destruction of her flat and triggered her stroke. But I couldn't think why Elsa wouldn't have returned Mum's belongings, including her diary – if, indeed, it had survived. I was positive we would have found it in her old flat, and Mum had already searched her new apartment from top to bottom.

Finding and questioning Elsa Kohl was my last resort. Why was this so important to me? Why could I not let it rest, as Helmut had suggested so many times? The research for my book – exploring the war's end though eyewitness accounts – strangely had coincided with the discovery of primary sources relating to my own family. And finding out the truth about Mother's role in the Nazi Party aroused an irresistible curiosity in me. Above all, I wanted to know whether the diary would reveal a change in attitude towards the end of the war. Would she at any stage have questioned her own role in the BdM? Or would she, like so many, have been in denial right to the bitter end?

'Another coffee?' I asked Mother when she came back. I had read somewhere that caffeine may help to strengthen long-term memory. She looked upset as she sat down again.

'All my things …' Her sentence trailed away in an exasperated sigh. 'All my things are still with her. She just wanted to type it up for me, wanted to do me a favour.'

'What things, Mum? What did she—?'

'The diary, *my* diary,' she interrupted, 'and some of our wedding photos, which she rescued from the flames. I wanted to show them to you. I can't find them, Jonas. Did she bring me the flowers? I gave them back to the nurse. I don't want her flowers. I want all my things back, Jonas. Can you tell her, please?'

She pushed her coffee cup further away and folded her arms angrily across her chest.

'I brought one of your lovely wedding photos.' I tried to calm her and reached for my rucksack. 'You probably won't remember, but you left me Grandma's old cigar box with lots of memorabilia. And that's where I found the wedding photo. Look – how beautiful! You in your white wedding dress, holding a wonderful bouquet of white roses, and

Dad in his smart uniform.'

Her face lit up. She pored over the photo, putting one hand on her heart and placing her other on top of mine. She was smiling again.

'He looks handsome there, doesn't he?' She hesitated for a moment before carrying on. 'Very different to when he came back from the war,' she added with a frown. She let go of my hand and began picking at the skin on her thumb. 'He was in a terrible state, you know. Half-starved, his feet blistered and infected from weeks of marching, blood-soaked bandages round his thigh … Terrible. But we were so happy. We fell into each other's arms and sobbed our hearts out. I shall never forget that day. It was the happiest day of my life: 30 May 1945.'

I shot a glance at her, wondering whether she was still comfortable with me dragging her back to a time of both happy and difficult memories. But all this burden of past experience did not seem to depress her. Quite the contrary. To my consternation, she began to recall long-buried details of Dad's narrow escape from becoming a prisoner of war. All of a sudden, she was lucid, as I had never seen her before, surprising me with remarkable feats of long-term memory.

'Two days after Rudi found us in Ernsthausen, the Americans knocked on our door, wanting to see his discharge papers. Of course, he didn't have any. We knew that officers would be sent to the notorious Stalag IX-B prison camp in Hesse. Since he didn't speak much English, I offered to interpret and was allowed to accompany him to the military government's office, where he was due to be interrogated. We couldn't believe our luck when the government officer's secretary stepped into the hallway calling Dad's name. I shouted, 'Marianne, good Lord!' She was an old BdM friend. We laughed and hugged each other. She didn't hesitate for one moment. She issued Rudi with a registration card and, instead of her boss's signature, stamped it with his facsimile. We scarpered, unnoticed, through the back door.'

'So how did you manage to get back to Dad's parents in the end?' I was curious to know.

'Well, of course the temporary registration card prohibited us from leaving Ernsthausen, but Rudi "persuaded" a lorry driver to take us to Leichlingen, near Cologne. In the middle of the night, we fled from the American zone, with our baby and Mother, into the British military zone. There, we were united with Rudi's parents and his brother, who'd survived the war unscathed. Everybody loved Helmut. We called him our little prince.'

I had no reason to doubt Mum's detailed story, and yet, as a historian, I was always on the lookout for corroborating evidence. Helmut had told me that juries tend to pay close attention to eyewitnesses' testimony and generally find them a reliable source of information. But their accounts can also be affected by psychological factors, such as anxiety, leading questions or memory lapse. 'I always treat a participant's own explanation of events with a certain degree of scepticism. They generally have their eye on the future outcome,' he had warned me.

They say time finds you out – you just need to dig deep enough. Dad had indeed narrowly escaped interrogation, and Mum, at some stage in the distant past, had given her diary to her friend Elsa, to be typed up. However, it wasn't clear to me whether the diary was ever returned to Mum and consequently lost, or whether, for some reason, Elsa had chosen to keep it. My photos had helped me to develop some aspects of my parents' past, but they still left important questions unanswered.

Mum fell asleep in the car on the way back to her home. I retrieved her bunch of flowers from the nurse, bought her a selection of Kinder chocolates from across the road and put both of them on her bedside table with a card – *With love from Jonas.*

I took a taxi back to Helmut's, excited and eager to tell him what I had discovered.

'I know there is no corroborating evidence for Mum's story. But there is no reason why Mum would invent or embellish an event like this. Don't you think?'

'It's true. Dad once told me about his narrow escape, but not in this much detail. He'd only mentioned it because I asked him why he, as an officer, had never been interrogated. With regard to the diary, I very much doubt it still exists.'

Then, like a surprise move in a chess game, he brought a box file down from his study, then presented me with the original registration card, dated 7 June 1945, which he had found when he was clearing Mum's flat. There it was – primary source material in black and white:

Military Government of Germany.
The holder of this card is duly registered as a resident of the town of Ernsthausen and is prohibited from leaving the place designated. Violation of this restriction will lead to immediate arrest.

It bore Dad's signature, the American officer's facsimile and even Dad's fingerprint. In the rush to issue the document, Mum's friend had entered *Medical doctor* instead of *Student of medicine* as his occupation.

'Dad would have loved that,' I said.

'Yes, I know. I'm not sure why I kept it. Here you are – take it with you. I don't want it back.'

Chapter 9

The next morning I caught the 7.45 train to Bad Iburg. I'd arranged to meet the two eyewitnesses, Mrs Rau and Mr Felz, who still lived in Mum's former Vivat home and had contributed their stories to *Days of Fear*.

Cologne train station was heaving with rush-hour commuters. The hubbub of sounds echoing around the main hall, and the hustle and bustle of the crowds, was only partially alleviated by the smell of freshly baked bread. I checked the timetable for the right platform, then followed my nose to the bakery.

With a paper cup of coffee in one hand and a huge croissant in the other, I sat down for an early breakfast on the platform. Like a pair of elderly Queen Victorias in mourning, two short, rotund ladies, covered in black headscarves, approached slowly, clearly looking for seats where they wouldn't have to sit near foreigners or be forced to listen to music blaring out of headphones. Settling down on the bench next to me, they gave me a disapproving look for eating in public.

'It's already two minutes late,' one of them moaned as the train nosed smoothly into the station's permanent twilight at 7.47. Within a minute, it had swallowed up all the waiting passengers, except for the two Victorias, who, for some reason, carried on chatting animatedly on their bench. After three beeps and a warning to stay back, the train began to move at a crawl, along its long platform with billboards of smiling young couples. Gradually, it gathered speed, lost the urban housing estates and cut through frozen countryside.

What puzzled me on the train, checking my notes after visiting Mum, was her mention of the notorious Stalag IX-B prison camp near Ziegenhain. She thought Dad would have ended up there had he not been able to evade capture. Googling it on Helmut's computer, I found that *Stalag* stood for *Stammlager* (prisoner-of-war base camp) – an overcrowded and squalid camp housing up to 25,000 prisoners from France, Great Britain, the Soviet Union, Belgium, Slovakia and the United States. The inmates were employed as forced labourers in agriculture, forestry and industry. In fact, Russian prisoners of war were treated most harshly, and many of them died. When the Allies turned the tables and used Stalag IX for German prisoners of war, Mum must have assumed they'd meet with the same fate. Had she also known about the existence of Groß-Rosen – the place where the photo of Dad, Elsa and her husband was taken? Should I ask her?

Bad Iburg is a quiet little spa town, near the Teutoburg Forest. There's not much to see apart from the castle, a clock museum and a former Benedictine abbey. I took a short cut from the station, leading past a half-frozen pond covered by a thin layer of ice. From an iron bridge, a man was throwing bread on to the icy surface. Dim, almost invisible through the dense fog, ducks nearest the shore waddled clumsily on the ice. Others, from further afield, flew towards the icy runway and landed with outstretched feet on the slippery surface. As I passed the elderly gentleman, he announced, pointing, 'That's what I call an elegant landing', then doffed his hat and smiled a farewell.

I'm not sure what motivated my parents to move here, apart from the fact that Vivat had been an award-winning home offering 'assisted living'. It was purpose-built with all amenities you could wish for in old age – except maybe a pool. The lady on Reception told me that my first meeting, with Mr Felz, had been arranged in the visitors' lounge on the ground floor.

Before I knocked, I inhaled and exhaled slowly a few times; it was the second time I had stood at the door of an unfamiliar eyewitness, not knowing what was in store for me.

Mr Felz was a tall, distinguished-looking old man, athletic in build, with silver-grey wavy hair and a moustache to match. In his navy-blue suit he looked a bit like a film star waiting to be interviewed. On his feet he wore a pair of shabby carpet slippers trodden down at the heel. An oversight, when compared to his otherwise immaculate attire?

'I'm very pleased to meet you, Mr Berger.' He greeted me with a firm handshake. 'How is your dear mother?'

'She's very well, thank you.'

'She was a great inspiration to us here and persuaded me to join the group, although I'm by no means a talented writer. Flying planes is more my thing – I used to be a Luftwaffe pilot. When I heard that you wanted to talk to me, I took another look at my story in *Days of Fear* and it all came flooding back to me. I can probably give you some more details now.'

'I'd love to hear your story, Mr Felz. Do you mind if I take some notes on my laptop?'

'Not at all. Take a seat and help yourself to coffee and biscuits.'

He cleared his throat and took a cigarette out of a silver case.

'We're not allowed to smoke here – anywhere,' he said with a mischievous smile, tapping the cigarette on his thumbnail and then lighting up. 'But I switched the air con on before taking off, so that's alright,' he laughed.

'Well, I'm taking you back to 1943. It was a few days before Christmas, and the Allied bombing campaign in Germany was going at full tilt. I had just been made Second Lieutenant, a freshly minted pilot, and was about to embark on my first mission to prevent the British from bombing our V1 and V2 rocket station at Peenemünde. Three of us, all flying single-pilot Messerschmitt Bf 110s, were scrambled at 04.45 on 26 August and sent to the radar station nearby. Unfortunately, the radio became jammed and we lost contact, so we didn't receive any information about the enemy position.'

He looked slightly agitated and puffed on his cigarette. I couldn't decide whether he was feeling anxious or excited.

'We climbed to about three and a half thousand metres over Peenemünde, when I suddenly spotted three Lancaster bombers just ahead of us, about five hundred metres below. I dived down, picked the one nearest to me and fired from a distance of about fifty metres. The enemy's engine two caught fire. As I broke away under the bomber, the rear gunner gave me a burst, but missed me – luckily. From the start of the attack, all three Lancasters were exposed to the German searchlights. As the other two aircraft tried to escape, my colleagues in their Messerschmitts pursued them in a pincer movement. They didn't stand a chance. They were hit, went into a spiral and crashed to the ground, a few hundred metres from the coastline. None of the crew survived.'

Why was he telling me this? This kind of dogfight was common in the war, resulting in huge, tragic losses on both sides. There was nothing heroic about it. It reminded me of a scene in Dad's old ciné film, where he was talking about the destruction of an enemy plane – and, of course, of our Latin teacher, who used to boast about the number of planes he'd shot down.

I stopped taking notes and poured myself another coffee. Unperturbed, Mr Felz continued with his story.

'When I descended, I saw the Lancaster I'd hit on my scope making a steep northwest turn towards Denmark. Smoke was coming out of its fuselage. I kept my distance, always taking care to stay out of his firing line, in case the guns were still in service. I then managed to fly within ten metres of the bullet-riddled Lancaster. I was aghast at the amount of damage the bomber had sustained. Its nose cone was missing and it had several gaping holes in the fuselage. I could see one crew member giving first aid to the wounded, but wasn't sure how many of the crew were still alive. I tried to contact the pilot using hand signals. "Land your plane in Denmark – I'll follow." He had no choice, and eventually crash-landed on the coast of southeast Jutland, about twenty-five kilometres north of the German border.

'When I arrived at the scene, one of the bystanders – a Danish man, known to be a Nazi sympathiser – kicked the injured captain lying on the ground, shouting, "Damned

English swine!" I turned round and hit the man with all my force, so that he tumbled to the ground. "Stop!" I shouted. "Leave him alone! He's a fair adversary." We gave the crew a decent burial in Aabenraa Cemetery.'

Mr Felz carried on for a while, describing in detail what happened to the captain – that he became a prisoner of war, but was treated fairly and with respect; that he returned home five months later, when British troops under Field Marshal Montgomery liberated Denmark.

What made him choose this story to tell me? One about toned-down heroism, throwing in a tinge of fairness just for good measure? A story about humanity in the horrific theatre of war – not unlike the 1914 Christmas truce football game between English and German troops? Was it stating that, even in war, we can display humanity?

How do they differ, the accounts in history books and the stories others tell us about *their* war experiences? Which come closer to the truth? Or is it simply a matter of primary over secondary sources? Are we really an authority on ourselves? But, as a historian, that isn't the question that concerns me most. The point is, eyewitness stories aren't really about what is true or false, about a more or less malleable past, but about attitudes and emotions inherent in the narrative, and how these change over time. Reliving the past is more like an open-ended journey – ultimately, one never finds proper closure. The soul is hardly a place for facts. To save his soul, had Helmut already opted to ignore the facts of our family history? Was he concealing any more vital evidence? Would I, also, have to choose between love and truth eventually?

For our book, Sam and I had classified the eyewitness accounts into five different categories (Mr Felz's story, like many others, fitted neatly into the second):

1. Victimisation – 'we lost everything and suffered just as much'
2. Justification – 'we did the best under the circumstances and showed some humanity'
3. Distancing yourself – 'we weren't really involved'
4. Being overpowered – 'there was nothing we could do'
5. Being fascinated – 'there were also good times' (e.g. BdM, no unemployment).

The Vivat cafeteria was a cacophony of loud chatter. On each table, a huddle of elderly people were raising their voices to be heard, some fiddling with their hearing devices. The food on their plates looked limp and uninviting. There were no prepared sandwiches on the counter. Reluctantly, I opted for the last dish of Bratwurst and potato salad.

I was still looking for a place to sit down when a projectile of boiled sweets shot towards me. An old lady in fancy dress had burst through the kitchen swing doors shouting, 'Kamelle' (sweets) and 'Strüßjer' (bunches of flowers), prematurely celebrating the carnival season. It's the sort of thing that's thrown into the crowds from floats during February's carnival procession in places like Köln or Düsseldorf. It's the time of year when, assisted by plenty of booze, Germans follow orders to be merry for a few days. Without delay, she was gently escorted out by one of the dinner ladies.

'She does this every week,' one of the men explained,

looking at my rather perplexed face. 'Highly entertaining, don't you think?'

After lunch, it was time to meet Mrs Rau. I'd opened the windows for a moment, wanting to clear the visitors' room of the cigarette smoke. The second I'd closed them, she knocked on the door. A buxom, grey-haired woman with rosy cheeks – I would say in her late seventies – she looked like a farmer's wife in a children's reading book. Mrs Rau unwound her scarf, shrugged off her coat and sat down opposite me. She wore gold-rimmed reading glasses, which, when not perched on the bridge of her nose, reposed on her large bosom, suspended from her neck by a gold chain. After a few introductory questions regarding Mother's state of health, she took out a copy of *Days of Fear* and opened it on the page of her contribution, 'My 21st Birthday'.

'My memory is not what it used to be, I'm afraid. I sometimes have to take a look to remind myself.'

'Of course. No problem at all.'

'Not many people want to hear about the war these days. And, for children, the war seems as remote as the Middle Ages. They need to hear from us what it was like living through it. And, when we've gone, from the next generation. That's why we wrote these stories down.'

'I agree. It's an excellent idea that the writing group recorded their experiences for future generations. But, please, you can tell me your story in your own words. Don't worry if it's not exactly as you've recorded it.'

She nervously nodded her head all the time during our initial conversation, took a sip of coffee from her cup and began without looking at her script.

'There are days and events in your life that stay with you forever. It was the spring of 1944. It was a lovely sunny day, 12 May – my birthday! I was still living in my parents' house in Osnabrück. All the fruit trees were in full bloom, spring flowers everywhere. It felt like a welcome distraction from the hardship and the daily bombing raids. My colleagues in the office didn't forget my birthday and gave me a large homemade birthday card and a bunch of spring flowers. Very sweet of them. In the afternoon, we had to join the *Arbeitsdienst* (enforced labour) to clear the rubble from the collapsed buildings – the men in the office often called us *Trümmerfrauen* (rubble women). Later on, we celebrated my birthday with family, and my best friend Ursel and her brother Günther, who lived nearby in Leyerstraße. They gave me a pair of nylon stockings, which Günther had brought back from France – a very special present at the time. My mother had made a rhubarb birthday cake. What a treat! I felt really spoiled. What happened in the evening, though, isn't easy to put into words …'

She paused, took a handkerchief out of her bag and blew her nose. Searching for the right words to continue, she perched her glasses on the bridge of her nose and ran her fingers down the second page of her chapter.

'The sirens started to wail. The nearest air-raid shelter was three kilometres away, so Ursel and Günther rushed home. Our family scarpered down into the cellar, where we had a few makeshift beds and kept provisions for a couple of days. We had a very close shave. We'd hardly shut the heavy metal cellar door when the house next to us took a direct hit. We could feel the tremors like an earthquake –

everything was shaking and rattling. Lime was crumbling down from walls and ceilings. The electricity cut out and we're sitting in the dark. My mother lit a candle. She tried to calm us and said: "Try and get some sleep till the all-clear." But we couldn't sleep. It was cold and damp. It was impossible. We were constantly listening out for the next bomb to hit our street, perhaps *our* house. Yes, we were lucky to have found shelter in time, but what went through my mind was whether we'd be able to get out alive or be buried under the rubble. And then, of course, you also had to remember that there were still people outside, being blown to bits by low-flying British bombers, who shot at anything that moved.'

Brief mental fact check: strategic bombing on both sides did indeed sometimes affect civilian areas, and some campaigns were deliberately designed to target the civilian population, specifically to terrorise and defeat enemy morale.

Mrs Rau's voice had taken on an exasperated edge. She breathed deeply and dabbed her tearful eyes.

'Several hours later, the all-clear finally sounded. I wanted to know whether Ursel and her brother were safe. When we stepped outside, we were confronted with an extraordinary sight: in the middle of the night we could see right up to Rubbenbruchsee, and all you could see around the lake were skeletons of buildings, everything in flames. What will remain in my memory forever, though, was the lake, which was literally on fire. All the burning buildings were reflected in the water. It was eerily beautiful and terrifying at the same time. Hundreds of incendiary bombs had been dropped on the most densely populated part of the town, and the whole sky was ablaze.'

'And were your friends safe?' I interrupted, gripped by her story.

'I walked up to Leyerstraße. There was no traffic. In the middle of the road a couple of women were singing their heads off and dancing in the street. "We are alive," one of the women shouted. "We have defied death," cried the other. People emerged from their cellars and everybody helped to clear up as quickly as they could. They started chatting, as if nothing had happened. And then I saw it: Leyerstraße 31. There was a large gap where Ursel and Günther's house had once stood. They had been buried alive under heaps of rubble and twisted metal, as was confirmed the next morning. It was terrible, absolutely terrible. I cried an awful lot. The whole family – Ursel, Günther, their sisters, aged ten and twelve, parents and grandparents – all lost their lives in one single night.'

There was a long silence in memory of her loss.

When I saw that her breathing had somewhat normalised, I said quietly, 'Thank you so much, Mrs Rau, for sharing this tragic story with me.'

On the way back to her flat (I thought it courteous to accompany her), she stopped in the corridor and handed me her copy of *Days of Fear*.

'I believe it's in good hands with you,' she said, placing her hand over mine. 'My daughter has a copy anyway. There are some stories in it with a happier ending than mine – like your mother's.'

I thanked her profusely, wondering whether I should try asking her about Elsa Kohl's whereabouts.

'I gather that not all contributions were published,' I

added, hoping she would mention Elsa voluntarily.

'That's right, but only one was rejected outright, and for a very good reason. Mrs Kohl was an incorrigible Nazi, and wrote a story glorifying her time in the BdM. I shouldn't really say that, because I think she was friendly with your mother. Anyway, she's gone now; she moved abroad.'

'And you never heard from her again?'

'Only once – about a year after she'd left. She sent me a postcard from England, raving about her "mansion", set on some famous London canal. It was probably just one of her many fantasies.'

I couldn't believe my luck. At home, I'd already searched the London phone directory in vain for an entry under Elsa Kohl's name. If true, the mention of a mansion house by a canal could be a vital clue. Another piece in my complicated jigsaw? So far, I'd been learning things in piecemeal fashion and many questions remained unanswered. I now needed to go back to my mind-mapping drawing board.

On the train back to the airport, I opened up MindManager on my laptop. It's a piece of software that I'd been using for my book research, and recently also for following up and connecting the various strands of my family research. Now, it needed updating.

Following up on Mum's single diary page and the photos on Dad's film roll, I now had a slightly better, but still opaque, idea of his involvement in the war and how he had escaped arrest. Mum had recognised her BdM friend Elsa and the SS man as her husband; Sam had identified the photo's location as the Groß-Rosen concentration camp; and Helmut had passed on Dad's letter about his tragic near-death experience. I still didn't have any detail about Elsa and her husband, other than the fact that she wasn't popular in the writing group and was possibly even now an unrepentant Nazi. If Mum was to be believed, her diary would still be with Elsa, who was now living somewhere in London in a 'mansion' by a canal. Thanks to Mrs Rau, I now had a copy of *Days of Fear*, containing many more eyewitness accounts and giving us ample material for our book.

How many famous canals are there in London? And was Elsa really living in a mansion?

Chapter 10

I had no lectures on Monday, but wanted to meet up with Sam to tell him my news.

'Regent's Canal is London's most famous, isn't it?' I asked him over lunch in the cafeteria.

'That's a bit random. Why? What about your trip? Any more eyewitness interviews?'

'Sorry. Yes, lots of news. Two more – I'll email you the transcripts. And what do you think of this?' Wiping the crumbs off the table, I pushed *Days of Fear* towards him.

His eyes were like two bright floodlights when he opened the contents page. I didn't have to draw his attention to Sarah Goldberg's story; he'd spotted it instantly. A heartbreaking account of Sarah, a Holocaust survivor born in the notorious Austrian Mauthausen-Gusen death camp. Miraculously, she and her mother survived to tell their story.

He looked up briefly, shaking his head. Then he read the opening sentence out loud: 'I'm not just telling a story, I'm talking about my family, most of whom were killed.' Taking a deep breath, he continued: 'I'd better read this at home.'

'Of course. Sorry. Take the book with you – by all means.'

'I still don't get it. What's all this got to do with canals?'

'Sorry. Yes … One of the eyewitnesses from the Vivat home received a postcard from my mother's friend, Elsa. Remember the photo of the BdM woman and the SS man?'

'The one in front of Groß-Rosen camp?'

'Yes. Elsa wrote in her postcard that she now lives in a mansion by a famous London canal.'

'Not much of a clue, is it? But I suppose it must be Regent's Canal. It's lined with enormous houses owned by the rich and famous. Is she that well-heeled?'

'I don't think so. Mother always referred to the Kohls as their "poor neighbours".'

'Well, there you are. Look, I know how much you want to find your mother's diary, but there may be other ways you—'

'No, you're right. I got a bit carried away.' I started gathering up our paper cups and empty sandwich boxes.

Sam made a move to leave and held up the book. 'Thanks for that. That's good: more primary sources. Oh, before I forget, can you remind your students to come to Friday's debate on Goldhagen's *Hitler's Willing Executioners*? Details on the History notice board.'

'Sure. I've already given them excerpts from Browning's *Ordinary Men* and asked them to read his reply to Goldhagen.'

I took a detour on the way home and cycled along Regent's Canal. I'd planned to start near Camden Lock, then move towards Limehouse, the cheaper end of the canal. Before setting off I went to the library to take a brief look at the history of London's canals. Apparently, Regent's Canal runs from Paddington to Limehouse; it's eight and a half miles long and, as the name suggests, dates from the early nineteenth century.

I soon swapped the busy streets for a behind-the-scenes view of London – rows of splendid houses on one side, backs of restaurants and warehouses on the other. Tethered to the banks of the canal was a demonstration of an alternative lifestyle – narrowboat living. What kind of person would choose to live on water in winter? There was a glimmer of light in one of the fancier boats. Through drawn curtains, I could make out the silhouette of a tall woman.

I pedalled slowly upstream along the towpath, unsure of my direction. Not knowing what to look out for, I briefly stopped near some less impressive mansions, but then discarded my futile idea altogether. This was going nowhere. A bitterly cold gust brought me back to my senses. Back into first gear, pedalling hard against the elements.

I cycled slowly alongside a low-lying barge, stacked high with heavy crates, a small tugboat towing it in the direction of Camden Market.

When I reached the Market Square, it was buzzing with people, like busy ants crisscrossing unpredictably. Some were stopping at food stalls to stock up on provisions; others were seeking gift inspiration at the Christmas stalls. I dismounted and stepped into the centre of the square. A street artist, kneeling on the pavement, was putting the final touches to a colourful chalk painting: a six-pointed star imprisoned in a circle. I was the only one who stopped to look. It reminded me of the Warsaw ghetto in the grip of freezing winter, still displaying a deceptive air of innocence, where an extra blanket would spell the difference between life and death. Then I thought of it as the centre of my family research, each star section pointing to an unanswered question. Questions that were far beyond my reach. I was ready to give up my quest for truth, but my soul was still not at ease.

What did you know about the crimes in Groß-Rosen, Mother? You must have recognised where that photo of Dad and Elsa was taken. Did you ever mention the concentration camp in your diary? When did you stop singing 'Uns're Fahne flattert uns voran' Our flag is flying in front of us? And, while you were living with her in the Vivat home, didn't you know why Elsa was planning to move to London? Do you have her address stashed away somewhere in your room? Why would she have held on to your diary?

Back on the towpath, past Stables Market, I slowed down to overhear a father explaining something to his young children: 'You see, the stables were important for the canals, because the boats used to be pulled by horses, which is why the canal has towpaths on either side. And the horses needed somewhere to sleep.' The children seemed more interested in the two ducks swimming upstream against the current. They appeared to be gliding effortlessly through the water, as if propelled by some kind of outboard motor, but underneath their webbed feet struggled hard to make progress. As the young family came nearer, out of the blue the little girl decided to throw her doll towards the ducks. Hitting the water with a splash, it bobbed for a few seconds on the caressing waves before filling with water and sinking to the bottom. I didn't wait to hear the ensuing argument. Or the tears!

Why on earth had I come here in the first place? Even if, by some bizarre coincidence, Elsa had been standing outside her house or strolling along the towpath, I wouldn't have recognised her. She must have been seventeen or eighteen in the photo, a tall woman with blonde plaited hair, dressed in her BdM uniform. There was no way I could even imagine how she'd look today.

I mean, look at *me* now. I'm fifty-four. Although I'm still as lean as I was many years ago, when I first walked across campus as a young lecturer, time has not been kind to me. My face looks more and more like tanned leather, and no longer stretches tautly over my sharp cheekbones. Thin lines have appeared around my mouth and eyes. And my hair, once light brown, has darkened with touches of grey around the temples.

I haven't had a serious relationship since Lucy left me three years ago, nor am I in the mood to start all over again. What's the point? Besides, I'm too busy, with teaching, marking and research for the book. I'm not afraid of the future. I have a sense of purpose, but I should never have started this bloody family research business. Look where it has led me: completely stuck, with the most vital questions unanswered. I should have listened to Helmut's warning when he handed me the box of memorabilia – 'Just leave the past *in* the past.'

The next morning, after my nine o'clock lecture, I sat in the library trying to find some peace and quiet so I could mark a pile of end-of-term assessments. Once I'd worked my way through the first half of the scripts, I leaned back, utterly exhausted, and stared at the grey partition wall in front of me. It seemed like only a short time had elapsed since I had started marking, but a glance at my watch told me otherwise. God – almost 12.30. My appointment with the Dean! Scrambling to my feet, I hastily gathered the students' assessment papers and hurried out of the library. Even though it was too late to make much difference, I sprinted across the campus to the Dean's office. His secretary stopped me with a wry smile and said, 'Professor Dyer-Sykes waited nearly twenty minutes for you. He's gone to the Senate House for an early lunch.' I assumed he'd wanted to ask me whether *Fractured Lives* was still going to be published in time for the next Research Assessment Exercise, for which the university attracts funding for future projects. Sam and I would have to work hard to meet that deadline.

Once home, I drafted a quick apology email to the Dean, assuring him that everything was on schedule – a little white lie. Then, having finished the rest of my marking, I started to tidy up my study. I wanted to draw a line under the family history. I had no real appetite to pursue it any further. One of the first things I removed from my desk was the old cigar box. I resisted the slight temptation to open Pandora's box again and banished it to the top bookshelf, which could only be reached with a stepladder. Had I missed any vital clues?

I used to begin my welcome lecture to the first years with: 'Why do we study history? Every time we try to understand why something happened – the dissolution of the British monarchy under Cromwell, or Hitler's rise to power, or the current Iraq war – we have to look for factors that took shape earlier on. We look for causes and effects that help to explain how and why events happened. And, most importantly, we try to see the past through the eyes of the people who lived it.'

To some extent, I had been able to see my family's history through my parents' eyes. But I'd failed to explore the depth of their involvement in the war. And the trail to Elsa Kohl, my most important eyewitness, had gone cold.

The microwave in the kitchen had just pinged to announce that my 'Beautifully Balanced Red Thai Chicken Curry' was ready, when the answerphone clicked into action. I opened a bottle of red and sat down with my dinner and the evening paper. I was in no mood to receive a rollicking from the Dean for not turning up, so it wasn't until much later that I listened to the message.

In fact, there were two. One from Sam, saying that he'd found Sarah Goldberg's story so very moving, and there was lots of other good material in *Days of Fear* we could include in our book. The second message was from Helmut and sounded worrying: 'Hi, it's me. Ring me back as soon as possible. It's urgent.' I tried his landline. No answer. As soon as I put my mobile on the table, it moved and lurched towards the edge. *Bzzzzt!* I caught it just in time. Helmut.

'Hi, I tried calling you – several times – but had to leave a message. Mum was taken into hospital again last night. I spoke to the senior consultant today. He said that she hasn't got long. Her heart's very weak and she may have suffered another stroke.'

My heart missed a beat at the news. 'Should I come over?'

'If you can. You never know …'

'It's the last week of term, but if you—'

'Up to you.'

'OK, I'll take the first flight tomorrow. I'll let you know when I'm getting in.'

I didn't sleep much that night. I felt guilty that I'd taken her back to that horrendous scene at the end of the war. I had made her relive her time in the air-raid shelter, which had triggered her first stroke. When we hurt a loved one, we hurt ourselves. I so wanted her to live … We'd always been close and I was forever grateful for her unconditional love. Was I just about to be confronted with the same dilemma as Helmut – choosing between love and truth? Yes, I had more questions to ask her, but I might not ever get another chance. The time for further questioning was finally over. I imagined her answering my Groß-Rosen question: *Well, you know, Jonas, in the middle of total war, you just went along with what you were told. You can only really understand these things if you lived through them. My primary worry was the safety of my girls, who'd been evacuated and were missing their parents – nothing else mattered.*

I arrived at the hospital the next evening. Helmut had stayed by her bed throughout the day, so I volunteered to do the night shift. As I sat down alongside her, a brief smile darted over her face, then faded away. She made no effort to talk. 'You're OK, Mum?' I took her hand and pressed it gently. I stared at the intravenous drip, not knowing what substances were being administered. The backs of her hands had turned purple from the numerous times blood had been taken from them. Her arms, folded across her chest, looked as thin as rakes. Her hair was lank, and her beautiful sapphire rings were almost falling off her fingers. The silence was broken only by the whisper of the young nurse who came in to check Mum's pulse. Time seemed to stand still for hours.

Suddenly, out of the blue, Mum began to speak in a low voice. She threw her sentence casually into the room like an item to be added to a shopping list.

'There's a new nightdress in the wardrobe – lovely material. Afterwards, you can give that to my friend Elsa.'

Afterwards? Mum! My stomach was churning. She didn't talk of dying. Oh no … She was calm and composed.

'That's all, my love, I'm so tired. Try to sleep yourself.' She closed her eyes.

I stumbled into the private room next door, desperate to get some shuteye. My head was spinning. Would she still be alive in the morning? Should I stay by her bedside?

I picked up a pen and started to write. I have never been any good at expressing my feelings. I'd never written a love poem for Lucy. Yes, I can write learned articles and academic books, based on proper research. But how does one research one's soul; put feelings into words? Where do people go when they die? Does their soul simply set up camp in our dreams?

The green digits on the radio clock in my room took ages to change from *03:25* to *03:26*. I could hear the ventilator pumping oxygen into the lungs of the patient next door and the beeping of heart monitors. I got up and asked the nurse for a sleeping pill, which eventually did the trick.

A knock on the door woke me up. Ten to eight. The

nurse called me.

'Come. Quickly. Your mother's heart rate has fallen.'

Mum's diaphragm hardly moved when she breathed. I inhaled deeply, breathing with her. She wanted to say something. Mumbles … just a few words. Names? I rested my hand gently on hers.

'I love you, Mum.' She pulled her hand away like a retracted promise, then took a few short, shallow breaths, one deep audible gasp inwards, followed by a protracted sigh. Silence. Nothing. The nurse wiped away a few tears. I sank into the chair by the bed and touched Mum's hand. It was still warm.

When Dad had died three years ago, it was Helmut who'd been the harbinger of sad news. And now it was my turn. When he entered the room, I just shook my head.

He gave me a stiff hug. Then, for a few moments, he stood grief-stricken and motionless by Mum's bed, as if petrified.

'She died peacefully,' I said, with a guilty conscience.

When he spoke, his tone was matter-of-fact, not accusatory. 'Do you know where she wanted to be laid to rest?'

'You mean, where she wanted to be buried?' I didn't like his euphemism. 'She wanted to be cremated and for her ashes to be scattered in the woods.'

'Are you sure?'

This was one of the rare occasions when *I* knew something about our parents that my older brother did not.

In the car on the way back, we were both left to our silent memories, retrieving last words, reliving recent visits, searching the depths of our memory for happy encounters. Helmut commented on the heavy traffic and pretended to concentrate on his driving.

'Can we talk through the arrangements and the service before I have to go back?' I asked.

'Sure. If you can get some ideas together for the service, I'd be grateful. I can do the rest.'

'I thought we'd just have a small gathering – family and friends.'

'Absolutely fine. I'll email you a list from her address book. And, Jonas … Feel free to add any names from her Vivat writing circle.'

Flying back to London, I wondered whether, one day, when asked about our Mother's past, Helmut would simply say: 'You know Jonas, for me, the mother chapter is now closed, too.'

For me, it felt more like a door had slammed shut in my face – one that I was desperate to keep open, or at least ajar. My family research had reached a dead end. It had released strong emotions in me, but it wasn't so much about catharsis, more about finding closure. If that's at all possible. And there *was* no closure.

At home, I scoured old photo albums and fished out pictures of her from the shoebox I'd taken from Mum's flat. I had envisaged putting together a kaleidoscope – arranged chronologically to present the patterns of light and shade in her life. I would scan the photos and project them onto a screen at the funeral to celebrate her life. Was 'celebrate' the right word? According to the *Shorter Oxford English Dictionary*, it means 'perform publicly and in due form any religious ceremony'. We were going to have a small, private gathering in Helmut's house, with no vicar. Curiously enough, under *Religion* on Mother's wedding certificate, it read, *God-fearing* – not *Protestant* or *Catholic*, as was the norm. I wasn't sure what 'in due form' meant. Did it imply that the celebration is conclusive, that no further evidence can be produced? Although I'd been able to shed some light on her time in the BdM, her war involvement was still inconclusive, unless we could find her diary ... and there was scant chance of that now.

A life laid bare in happy snaps on the living-room floor.

The smiley six-year-old schoolgirl, satchel strapped round her shoulders; the proud ten-year-old in her BdM uniform. Then I left a gap on the floor – there were no photographs of her for the period between 1933, Hitler's seizure of power, and 1940. In the next photo she's in her BdM leader's uniform – about seventeen, I would guess – looking after evacuated children in Lower Silesia. A pencil mark on the back of the photo says *1940*. Then, four years later, a few wedding photos. I added the one from the scrapbook in my cigar box, even though I had banished it to the top shelf in my study. Then, the happy couple smiling into the camera in front of a hastily erected screen, which only partially concealed the ruins and skeletons of bombed-out houses. Mum in her white chiffon dress with a modest V-neck, holding a large bunch of white roses; Dad in his officer's uniform with full regalia and peaked cap. We jump to 1947, the first snap of Mother and child.

She's playing the accordion, standing up and looking down at the keys, while little Helmut stretches up in an attempt to reach the lowest black key. Another early post-war snap shows our parents dressed to go out – she in a fur coat, he in an elegant black double-breasted coat over a white scarf, and wearing a top hat. Had they been able to hold on to their pre-war savings?

In a semi-circle, underneath the photographs, I laid out an array of holiday and leisure snaps. These were difficult to date. Mum and Dad on the tennis court with old-fashioned wooden rackets; pictures of walking, skiing and painting holidays. Seemingly beaming, happy faces – at times, a bit too cheesy for my liking. Conspicuous by their absence, however, were photos of a domestic nature. But then who wants to be photographed arguing at the dinner table over domestic chores or fighting over money. Phrases like 'Why do you always…?', 'Can you not…?' and 'You don't understand …' Accusations and door-slamming don't translate easily into photographs. However, they strike a different chord to the rosiness of the holiday snaps. Who am I to criticise? I'm sure they once had their love story. But at least, in my Dad's case, it was not the only story.

I pictured their life frame by frame, like in Dad's old 16mm ciné film: starting off together during the war, falling in love – the first man in Mum's life. Hastily getting married in 1944, with a child on the way, amidst the ruins of Cologne. Overcoming hardship and fleeing for their lives. Eventually, happily reunited after the war. Then, as life proceeds, in its prosperous, unthreatening way – the brown past having been cleansed away – they grow apart but stay together, for the children's sake, for our sake. To us kids, however troublesome or mysterious their past may have been, everything seemed normal. Indeed, the gradual realisation of their true past was a sign of our growing maturity, a chance to be different and develop our own personalities. But for them there was no escape: they would always be tainted by the brush of history, by the shadow of the high mound of brown earth threatening to entomb them. Now they were both safe ... or were they?

Helmut emailed me the date of the funeral – 18 December – along with a list of invited guests. He complained about his impersonal, businesslike treatment at the undertaker's.

'Everything is computerised these days,' he wrote. 'There's even a "death menu" to choose from, for heaven's sake.' What on earth was *that*? He didn't elaborate, but my mind boggled. Would it be some kind of upgrade on the usual sandwich and slices-of-cake lunch? Hemlock crunchy crudités for starters, followed by ...? Better not go there.

I ran my finger down Helmut's list of guests and spotted Elsa Kohl's name, highlighted with a question mark. Had he found her in Mum's address book? Why the question mark? Was he unsure whether to invite her, or did he not have an address for her? Had he met her when Mum was still alive?

Chapter 11

Just about everyone came. Everyone on the guest list that is – although, as expected, Lucy declined the invitation. She had never bonded with Mum. You could tell by the lack of bodily contact. She had developed this strange technique of hugging Mum without ever touching her, extending her arms stiffly as though she was hugging a large tree.

However, I was very pleased that Ludger, my stepson, had made the effort to attend. He's reading English at Edinburgh University. He comes to see me during his holidays and usually stays for a few days. We get on much better now that Lucy and I don't live together any more.

The funeral was a very different affair from any services I had attended previously. I was glad we weren't crammed into some old cemetery chapel, having to endure endless readings. There was no minister of religion running the show. We didn't have to stand and sing and pray, then sit and stand and sing again. We were all seated comfortably in a semi-circle in Helmut's large lounge, listening to a few short speeches given by family and friends, recounting anecdotes and happy memories.

We then watched the slide show I had put together – the collection of Mum's photos at different stages of her life. Some of them were met with deadly silence, while others, like little Helmut reaching up to press a key on Mum's accordion, evoked an upbeat *aah* reaction.

On a table in front of us, surrounded by a sea of

flowers, sat the urn, alongside an oversize black-and-white photograph of Mum. It was Helmut's choice – a little too grainy for my liking. She looked benign, yet somewhat pensive. There was an odd smudge of white powder on her face. Had she tried to wipe it off? She was never any good at applying make-up; never had much practice, I suppose. Hitler's phrase 'a German girl does not wear make-up' sprang to mind. History is like powder on your skin, I had read somewhere – you try to dust it off from time to time only to realise that it has already sunk irretrievably into your pores.

Later on, we congregated around the grave, dug the urn into the ground and performed the earth-to-earth gesture, while friends kept a tactful distance awaiting their turn. Against Mum's wish, we had decided not to scatter the ashes, but bury the urn in the local cemetery. I'm not entirely sure, but I thought I heard Helmut whisper a faint, almost imperceptible 'I love you, Mum' as he paid his last respects.

That evening, when everybody had left, we both slumped into comfortable armchairs, limp with fatigue and weary with the burden of too much emotion. The stillness was oppressive, like the awkward silence of an estranged couple, full of unacknowledged thoughts and hidden feelings.

Helmut broke the silence: 'Good turnout, I thought. I'm glad everybody could come.'

'Not everybody.'

'Who was missing?'

You had Elsa Kohl on your list with a question mark and you didn't answer my email when I asked about her.'

'I wasn't sure she should make the journey. She must be

about Mum's age.'

'How do you know she doesn't live here any more?'

He got up and walked over to the open-plan kitchen, stifling a yawn.

'Would you like some supper? I'm starving. I couldn't eat anything earlier on.'

'How do you know she doesn't live here any more?' I said, raising my voice. The adrenalin started to kick in. Frustration, rage, I don't know what I was feeling. Was there another secret he was hiding from me?

'Well, it's a long story. Come and help me cut up some vegetables.' He opened the cutlery drawer and handed me a large chopping knife. I grabbed the knife, clenched it tightly and slashed the air behind his back.

'Spit it out, will you! I want to know. I'm sick and tired of all your little secrets. For fuck's sake, do you know where she lives or not?'

'Steady on. I was about to tell you.' He chucked a few pieces of chicken into a hot sizzling pan, then turned round to face me. 'About a year ago, Mum asked me whether I could give her friend Elsa some legal advice. She was worried that she could be deported to Germany from England for crimes against humanity.'

'What crimes?'

'Well, she didn't kill anybody, but worked for about a year in what she described as a labour camp.'

'A concentration camp, more likely.'

'Possibly, I don't know,' he said shrugging his shoulders.

'I do. I have a photo of her, together with her SS husband and Dad, posing in front of the concentration camp at Groß-Rosen. She must have worked there.'

'All I know is that she worked in a camp, possibly as a guard. We don't know. Anyway, she was frightened of being charged as an accessory to murder.'

'So she should, don't you think? Clearly, there's a case for aiding and abetting. She would have been part of the whole killing machine … So she could still—'

'Look, I'm not a specialist in this field, and neither are you. When I checked the Criminal Code, I found that the statute of limitation for Nazi war crimes was abolished in 1979. So theoretically – under the European Convention on Extradition – she could still be extradited. However, as far as I understand, perpetrators can only be prosecuted if there are eyewitnesses; a paper trail is not enough. I explained this to her in a letter. I don't think she needs to worry too much.'

'Whose side are *you* on?'

'It was Mum's request. I only explained the legal situation to her. She now lives in London under the name of Clara Roberts. I found her new name under "R" in Mum's address book. In brackets, she'd written "Elsa".'

'And you think that people like her should never face judgment for what they did?'

'I didn't say that. I just explained the legal position.'

'Soon there will be no more Holocaust survivors left who have actually witnessed these atrocities. Isn't it enough to establish that she willingly served as part of the killing apparatus?'

'What's that smell?' Helmut suddenly noticed that he'd burnt the chicken and whisked the pan off the hob.

'Shit! For God's sake, Jonas, it's more complicated than that. Can we just finish preparing our meal first? We can continue this discussion over supper.'

I carried on slicing the vegetables more vigorously than I needed to, making excruciatingly loud chopping noises. A carrot, which tried to escape by rolling off the kitchen table, was executed on the spot. I felt a strange mixture of rage and relief. I was outraged, because this was yet another example of Helmut holding back vital information from me, and somewhat relieved and excited that I would now be able to trace Elsa and possibly find out what happened to Mum's diary.

Later on, Helmut explained to me at great length that prosecutors would first have to prove that the person's name on the list was the same as that of the person living today. Furthermore, they would have to prove Elsa was there for more than a day, and that she understood what was going on in the camp. They would also have to be certain that the crime had been motivated by racial hatred, a high standard that could be hard to establish without witnesses and firm evidence. And finally, the Court would have to determine that the defendant is fit to stand trial, which can be difficult in the case of elderly people. Given Elsa's age, her capacity to stand trial could change very quickly, so that a once promising case could overnight become impossible to prosecute.

I still felt that Helmut was using arguments that obfuscated the main issue of Elsa's guilt. In my view she was guilty, because as a guard at the camp she would have known what was happening there and thus played a part in the killing of thousands of prisoners. Would Mum have known that her friend had been working as a prison guard while she was looking after evacuated children? She'd once told me that Elsa was also sent to a children's evacuation camp near Liegnitz, but then Elsa may not have told her the truth. However, Dad must have known about her role in the camp. How well did he actually know her?

Elsa's silhouette had gradually taken on a sharper profile: Mum's friend and subordinate in the BdM was about seventy-nine or eighty years old; wife of SS officer Herbert Kohl, who was hanged for mass murder following the Nuremberg trials. She had fled to London for fear of arrest in Germany and changed her name to Clara Roberts. According to Helmut, she was now living at Doctor's House, 89 Manor Road on Regent's Canal. A small cog who had helped to keep the death machinery operating smoothly. She had gone on to lead a normal life, never facing judgment for what she did. I imagined her, now elderly and frail, being extradited and dragged from her anonymous post-war existence. Would she be deemed fit enough to stand trial?

I left Cologne the next day, as soon as Helmut and I had settled the bill for the funeral. There were a few thousand euros left in Mum's savings account, which we decided not to touch, in case the tax authorities discovered that she had unwittingly failed to pay tax on her pension for the last couple of years.

Ludger had already flown back to London the night before and was waiting for me when I got home. It made a nice change from coming back to an empty house. He'd decided to stay a few days until Christmas Eve and then spend Christmas Day with his mum. He had had another growth spurt. His face looked pale and bereft.

He showed me a picture of Mum on his phone. She was resting on a lounger on her narrow balcony, wrapped up in blankets, wearing a white bobble hat pulled right down to her eyebrows.

'I loved Oma,' he said, when we had settled down to a take-away dinner. 'I know she was very forgetful, but she still remembered that I was reading English at uni, proudly telling me about her favourite author, Aldous Huxley. She seemed to have read most of his books. Amazing, the details she could recall from *Brave New World*.'

'Yes, her long-term memory was pretty much intact. When, occasionally, she talked about her time in the BdM, I encouraged her to write down her memories – which she did. It's called *My Childhood and Youth in the League of German Girls of the Hitler Youth*. We found a copy when we cleared out her flat.

'I'd really like to read that. I know very little about the Hitler Youth.'

'Apparently, she also wrote a war diary. It may still exist and be at her friend's house here in London.'

'That would be amazing. You're writing about that kind of stuff, aren't you?'

'Yes, a colleague and I are preparing a book called *Fractured Lives*. It's an eyewitness account of the end of the Second World War.'

'We're studying First World War novels next term, like Sebastian Faulks' *Birdsong* and Erich Maria Remarque's *All Quiet on the Western Front*. It's so weird to think that Grandma and Grandad lived through a horrific world war.' He pushed his empty plate away, leaned forward and cupped his head in both hands. 'So, this friend of

Grandma's – she could be another eyewitness for your book. Are you going to meet her?'

'I'm a bit apprehensive about that. She won't want to talk about her past.'

'Why not?'

'She was working in a concentration camp in 1944. She may have been a guard there.'

'Really? Holy shit! Did Oma know about this?'

'I don't know, but her diary may tell us … If it still exists.'

'I can't believe she knew. She wouldn't have been friends with someone who was sending prisoners to their deaths. Surely not. Have you met this woman before?'

'No. But I have her address now.'

'So how will you find out the truth about her, and the whereabouts of Oma's diary?'

'I really don't know.'

'You could tell her that we wanted to invite her to Oma's funeral, but didn't have her address.'

Ludger was right. I needed a credible pretext for seeing her. But I also needed to have a strategy to ingratiate myself and put her off guard. She'd be suspicious of anybody wanting to delve into her past. And what about her niece? Would *she* know about Elsa's dark past? Why was she living with her aunt? Would she have come across the diary, stashed away in a secret hiding place?

I went upstairs into my study and switched on my PC. I typed Elsa's postcode into Google to see exactly where she lived. My screen froze unexpectedly – just as Sam rang. He had been concerned to hear that Mother had passed away and wanted to know how I was.

'The funeral went better than expected,' I said. 'Everyone was very supportive. And Ludger came as well; he's staying with me for a few days.'

'That's really good. It's so important to have family with you at such a difficult time.'

'I'm sorry I missed the Goldhagen debate on *Hitler's Willing Executioners*. How did it go?'

'Your students were great. They asked all the right questions. They were quite scathing about the lack of factual content and evidence for Goldhagen's main argument that there was unique widespread anti-Semitism in Germany. One of them drew attention to the lack of primary sources and the fact that Goldhagen's book didn't even have a bibliography. Your teaching has obviously not fallen on deaf ears.'

'I'm glad to hear that. There's something else I wanted to talk to you about: Do you remember my mother's friend, Elsa Kohl?'

'Yes, of course, from the picture at Groß-Rosen you showed me.'

'Well, I now have her address.'

'How come?'

'My brother had it all the time. It turns out that she'd most likely been working there as a prison guard.'

'Are you sure?'

'Almost certain, because she asked Helmut about the likelihood of her being extradited. And according to him – unless there were actual eyewitnesses – the chances are apparently very slim.'

'Hello?' I thought we'd lost the connection for a moment. 'Are you still there?'

'Yes. Hang on,' he said, his curiosity now thoroughly aroused. 'I thought, I read … wait a minute. I'll ring you back. I just need to check something.' He hung up. What was all that about?

'Bloody PC. Come on … where is it? I want to see where she lives,' I said to myself a few minutes later, as I rebooted while waiting for Sam to call back. His news came as a complete surprise.

'Listen to this,' he said quickly. 'It's from an article in the *Spiegel*, just two weeks ago. There's been a recent change in German law, approved by the German parliament with a slim majority: "You no longer have to prove an intentional act that directly leads to a killing", it says here, and "from now on, the mere presence and support of the whole system of a death camp is punishable".'

'Really? If that's right … Can we check with the Central Office for the Investigation of National Socialist Crimes in Ludwigsburg first, and then—'

'I'm sure the Wiesenthal Centre would also be interested in this case. I hope your brother isn't going to help Elsa any further.' His voice sounded slightly reproachful. 'Are you still going to visit her?'

'Yes, absolutely, I must find out the truth about her and ask her about my Mum's diary.'

'Just don't get your hopes up. She'll be very reluctant to talk about her past. You'll have to think of a pretty good game plan. Don't worry, we'll sort something out. You'll see.'

Had Helmut not told me the whole truth? Or was he simply not up-to-date and merely relying on the information from the outdated Criminal Code? Why would he not agree with me that people like Elsa, who were able to avoid punishment for so long, should now be brought to justice? At this late stage in history and against the backdrop of Holocaust deniers, we do need eyewitnesses like her. Sam and I agreed to meet after Christmas to discuss our strategy.

The next day, I cycled once more alongside Regent's Canal. It was a mild, drizzly day. There seemed no hope of a white Christmas. If the address Doctor's House, 89 Manor Road, wasn't curious enough, the house itself came as a complete surprise. As I approached it for the first time, this Gothic-style mansion had an air of decay and quiet discouragement. The old house seemed to have collapsed inwardly on itself, like a loaf of bread taken out of the oven prematurely. The roof had sagged in the middle, forcing some of the cedar shingles to stick up like wonky teeth. Many of the arched windows were boarded up, their frames rotten and surrounded by crumbling plasterwork. Water dripped down the sills onto the dirty cream cracked paint. The rounded porch, with a grotesque-looking gargoyle sitting on top, looked like a bad afterthought. A large spider was clinging to the gargoyle's open mouth with its ghostly fingers.

I took a stroll down a little footpath to get a view of the back of the house. The garden, wild and overgrown, was dotted with a few apple or pear trees. Bobbing in the puddles underneath, the rotten fruits were hardly recognisable. A few poles stuck out of the deep lawn, forming a rickety trellis on which climbing roses and clematis may once have grown. Strangely enough, the garden was unfenced –

it stretched down to the canal – and it suddenly occurred to me that if it didn't belong to the house, it would give me the perfect pretext to wander in and catch a clandestine glimpse of its inhabitants.

Suddenly, two young boys, no older than ten or twelve, appeared out of nowhere.

'Going to see the witch, are you?' The taller one took a step towards me. 'Do you want to know a secret?' He just stood there with his hand stretched out.

'What secret?'

'Give us a quid.'

'What would I give you a quid for?'

'For me to tell you what I know.'

'First the information, then the money.' I made a swift grab at the boy, but he was quicker and slipped through my arm.

'Forget it,' he shouted, mumbled some abuse and re-joined his friend. I made my way back up to the front of the house, when, after a few minutes, the same boy turned up again, this time without his friend. He had positioned himself near the entrance gate, cautiously standing some yards away. He said cheekily, 'It's two quid now for the secret. Price has gone up.' I wasn't sure what to do.

'Alright then,' I said reluctantly and offered him the money.

'No, you'll try to grab me again. I know you. Just leave the money on the gate post before you knock on the door.'

'Well?' I said, as I stood under the porch.

'The witch burns things in a cauldron when it's dark.' He swiftly grabbed the money and ran off. I could have got hold of the little squirt, but I withstood the temptation so close to the house. It wouldn't exactly have been a good introduction, if anyone inside had seen me grabbing the child. I dismissed the boy's comment as child's play, mere fantasy. He may have seen Elsa with a walking stick in the garden bending over an autumn bonfire.

I needed to keep a cool head, be friendly and impartial, or at least pretend to be. After all, she used to be Mum's friend. When I rang the rusty doorbell, I had no idea what to expect. Why did I feel a horrible sense of foreboding? A sense that something would go wrong?

'Who's there?' A woman shouted from a first-floor window. I stepped back from underneath the porch and looked up to see her face – pale, but pleasant looking. Her auburn hair was tied back in a ponytail.

'Sorry to disturb you. My name is Jonas Berger. I was hoping to speak with Mrs Roberts, who's an old friend of my mother.'

'Mrs Roberts is unwell. She can't see you,' she snapped, her hands reaching up to close the sash window.

'Wait! Could you just give her these presents, then? My mother wanted her to have them.'

The window slammed shut with a loud bang. Moments later, the front door opened, groaning and grating against the stone floor. The woman popped her head round the half-open door.

'Yes?'

'I'm sorry to come unannounced. I hope I'm not intruding. You see, my mother died recently, and I thought Mrs Roberts would want to know—'

'She's really not well,' her voice softened a little.

'I didn't realise. Would you mind giving her these

presents? My mother—'

'Yes, of course. I'm her niece. Bettina.'

'And might I be able to speak to her another time?'

'I'll ask her.' I had hardly been able to catch a glimpse of the badly lit hall when she pushed the door shut in my face. The niece had the demeanour of a woman who was capable of fending off any intruder like a guard dog.

Elsa agreed to see me early in the New Year. Her niece would ring me to arrange a mutually convenient date. Although I hadn't been able to penetrate their citadel, I had finally tracked them down and got my foot in the door with an appointment.

Sam had invited me for brunch on Boxing Day. Unlike mine, his was a house that breathed life, a house with toys on the stairs that smelled of coffee, cigarette smoke and perfume. The *Jewish Chronicle* and history books lay strewn over the coffee table. There were open CD cases on the shelves and a cat licking the butter on the breakfast table. Sam shooed the cat away and poured us coffee.

'Ruth and the children have gone to visit relatives in Hampstead. They'll be back in an hour.' I handed him a poinsettia for his wife and some presents for the children.

'Thanks, Jonas. They'll be delighted to receive even more presents.'

'I see you still play,' I said, pointing in the direction of the upright piano.

'A little, now and then. It reminds me of my grandad – he used to play. He survived a little longer in the camp, playing the piano while others were tortured.'

He watched me take a closer look at the piano music –

the *St Matthew Passion*.

'It's a source of hope,' he said. 'I wish that humanity might one day be a little more Johann-Sebastian-like.' To my relief, after a short pause, he changed the subject.

'Have you managed to check the information I gave you on statutory limitations?'

'Yes. The Central Office in Ludwigsburg confirmed that Nazi crimes are no longer time-barred.'

'So, what's the plan?'

'I've already been to Elsa's house.'

'And?'

'I only spoke to her niece, but have arranged to meet Elsa some time in a couple of weeks. She was unwell.'

'You won't find out much in a single meeting. Remember, she's afraid of being deported. She'll be very suspicious of you.'

'I know.'

'Also, she may have dementia. But even if not, she won't tell you anything.'

'What do *you* suggest, then?'

'You'll need to befriend the niece.'

'You mean, get to the old woman through her niece? And how would that work?'

He hesitated for a moment. 'Well, you're single, aren't you?'

'You mean—'

'Exactly.'

Bettina was a pleasant looking woman in her forties. I wasn't sure, though, whether it would be easy to get to know her and gain her trust. She was clearly very protective of her aunt and I would have to tame the guard dog inside her. However, I would also have to hatch a little plan to ingratiate myself with her aunt. Would Elsa ever be willing to talk to me about her past and reveal the whereabouts of the diary? I felt both anxious and uneasy at the prospect of befriending both ladies and gaining their confidence based on ulterior motives. And, looking back, the whole affair turned out to be far more complicated than I had envisaged.

Thanks, Sam!

Chapter 12

Three weeks later – the spring term had already started – I got a call from Elsa's niece. Introducing herself as Bettina Klein, her voice sounded so matter-of-fact, like a receptionist in a busy doctor's practice.

'Mrs Roberts sends her apologies for not getting in touch earlier. She forgot you called.'

'Not to worry. Thank you.'

'Oh, and … she's very sorry to hear about your mother. She doesn't normally receive visitors, but is keen to see you. You can come tomorrow afternoon at four, she says.'

I accepted the invitation immediately. I knew full well that I'd have to clear my diary and excuse myself from the weekly staff meeting.

But what could I achieve in a single visit? Sam had reminded me, quite rightly, that if I were to find an answer to all my queries – the diary, Elsa's past, her relationship with Dad – I'd need a longer-term game plan. I had to find a way to establish a relationship with her, if only temporarily.

I hesitated for a moment to ring the doorbell. Previously, I hadn't noticed the tarnished brass plaque above the door with its curious inscription, *The Doctor's House*. Perhaps this rather dilapidated mansion had once been a busy surgery. Why did it close down – did anything sinister happen here? I wondered whether this was a house full of untold stories.

Bettina answered the door and led me through a long hallway into what must once have been the living room. A strange smell wafted towards me – an odd mix of cleaning fluid and sweet tobacco. Clutching a bunch of flowers, I entered a cold, sparsely decorated room, its dominant feature being a large portrait of an Alsatian hanging on an otherwise empty wood-panelled wall. Would there be a German shepherd dog keeping me in check? I imagined the niece lobbing a half-eaten bone into the corner of the room to appease the beast. I scanned the room anxiously. No dog – phew!

I don't recall how I greeted Mrs Roberts, aka Elsa Kohl. I had rehearsed a few sentences about Mother – how much she would have liked to have stayed in touch, and that she'd often talked about their BdM times – and proceeded to recite them to her. A gaunt, birdlike woman in her late seventies, possibly early eighties, her white hair was coiled into a serpent-shaped bun at the back of her head, and she sat hunched in a winged armchair with a woollen shawl knotted round her shoulders. Oddly enough, she was smoking a meerschaum pipe. Her teeth, gripping the stem, had turned yellow; the fingers on her right hand were stained with red marker pen. Elsa looked like the kind of woman who'd outlived the majority of her relatives.

'So, you're Cäcilia's younger son,' she croaked, knocking a small compacted parcel of ash from her pipe into an overflowing ashtray. She looked me up and down like a guard deciding whether or not to let me in. 'You don't look a bit like your brother.' In the next breath she added, 'I'm so sorry to hear about your mother. We were good friends. I would have liked to come to the funeral, but your brother thought the journey would be too arduous, at my age.'

Her niece noticed that I was still standing forlorn in the middle of the room, not knowing whether or where to sit down. Bettina pushed a chair towards me, at some distance from her aunt's chair, and gestured for me to sit. It was one of those moulded plastic chairs you'd normally find in a doctor's waiting room. I then handed her the flowers, with a smile.

'Any tea or coffee?' she asked, acknowledging the flowers with a brief inclination of her head.

'My usual camomile, dear,' Elsa butted in before I could answer. 'And put the flowers in a vase, will you.'

'And, for you?'

'May I have a coffee, please? White, no sugar. Oh, and the flowers are for *both* of you.'

'They're lovely, thank you,' Bettina replied. The brief smile had faded from her face before she disappeared into the kitchen.

While Elsa was busy stuffing her pipe with fresh tobacco, I scanned the sparsely furnished room. The only furniture left in this large room was a blanket-draped sofa, a coffee table covered with piles of books and magazines, and an old-fashioned sideboard. They had placed a two-bar electric fire in the inglenook fireplace, in a forlorn attempt to take the chill off this huge expanse. Elsa reached over to the coffee table, grabbed a box of matches and began to light her pipe. The draft from the sash windows blew little puffs of smoke in my direction. What was she thinking? Did she suspect that my visit had an ulterior motive?

'Your mother and I were good friends,' she repeated, still drawing on her pipe to light it properly.

'She often talked about you. You go back a long time, don't you? Didn't you live on the same floor in the Vivat home?'

Elsa blew more puffs into the cold air, which hung between us like a milky cloud. Would she try to put up a smokescreen when questioned about her past? 'I don't remember. I think your mother was in a different home. She was my superior in the BdM, you know. She was a good leader.'

'I thought you were in the same writing group at Vivat?' I continued to probe. 'She said you were very talented at writing – diaries, life writing, your experiences during the war. Didn't you also write something for *Days of Fear*?' My compliment was a blatant lie, but it did the trick.

'Oh, that wretched book. They didn't include my contribution – they must have forgotten it somehow. I was quite upset about it at the time. Didn't even get a copy.'

'But you've got one now,' Bettina added, carrying in a tray of tea and coffee. 'Dr Berger left you a copy, along with the nightdress. Presents from his mother – remember? You were unwell when he called a few weeks ago.' She glanced up from the tray, rolling her eyes as if to say, She doesn't remember …

'Now, put that pipe away,' she continued, disapprovingly. 'Do you have to smoke when we have visitors? It's not very courteous, nor is it any good for you.' She moved the ashtray aside and put the cup of camomile tea in its place.

'But I like smoking,' Elsa retorted a little petulantly, then turned to me. 'And what brings you over here, Jonas? Are you in touch with Helmut?'

'Yes, I saw him at Mum's funeral, just before Christmas.

He's fine – he gave me your address and sends his regards. But I don't live in Germany any more. I've been living in London for more than twenty years now. I teach German History at University College London. My research—'

'Really?' Bettina interjected, suddenly seeming very animated. 'I work in the History and Classics Department at the British Library – part-time now. Sorry I interrupted you. What's your field of research?'

By some curious stroke of luck, we had something in common, something for me to build on. However, when I talked about our research for *Fractured Lives*, and mentioned that we were still trying to locate more eyewitnesses, her body language instantly changed. Bettina crossed her arms and pressed her lips together in a slight frown.

'It sounds like a very interesting project, but the problem with eyewitnesses is that they're prone to error and bias, don't you find? Especially when it comes to elderly people talking about their youth. We all forget things over time.'

'But what if those memories were written down at the time?'

'Even then … ,' she held back and left the sentence unfinished. I sensed that my question had somehow disturbed the fragile peace of our discussion.

Bettina perched on the edge of the sofa opposite the bay window – the heavy curtains were only half drawn. I watched the few beams of sunshine play on her face, contemplating whether she knew anything about Mother's diary. She had a pretty, oval-shaped face, brown eyes, auburn hair and a melancholy look about her that was strangely endearing. Like a hawk, Elsa followed every movement of her niece's eyes, as though she might let slip certain secrets if she did not hold Bettina with her gaze.

'Well,' she said, blowing a loose strand of hair off her face, 'most people don't want to be reminded of those horrible war memories, do they, Auntie? And we all forget things that happened so many years ago.'

What came next surprised and delighted me in equal measure. Completely unprompted, Elsa began delivering exactly that: an eyewitness account of what happened during the last year of the war. Like an unruly child, she was stubbornly defying Bettina's attempts to stop her discussing the past.

'Not all things,' she replied. 'Some you never forget. My eighteenth birthday – 2 August 1944. How long ago is that, Tina? Let me see – 2004 minus 1944. Sixty years ago. Goodness gracious! But I remember it as though it were yesterday. We'd celebrated my birthday in your mother's flat, Jonas. Ours had been bombed out several weeks before. We always had our bags packed ready for the air-raid shelter in the downstairs hall. Just with the basics – papers, money, jewellery, a change of clothes. Everyone did, as sometimes there were only minutes between the sirens and the bombs. Anyway, it was late evening when the sirens went off. We ran out across the road to the shelter. The first phosphorus bombs had just started to rain down on us, as though poured from giant buckets. With everybody rushing to the shelter and nobody to supervise, it was complete mayhem. People pushed and shoved in front of the entrance, trying desperately to get inside. Some didn't make it and were burnt alive. My uncle Ernst died in the flames. He'd let the children and women in first, bless him. Phosphorus can't be put out by dousing it with water, you see – we tried.'

Elsa coughed repeatedly, then took a sip of her camomile tea and leaned back in her chair, folding her hands in her lap. She stopped speaking for a moment and looked out of the window. Silence hung in the room for a fraction of a minute. Bettina shifted uneasily on her seat, then straightened her back. She was about to get up, to attend to her aunt.

'I think you should rest now. You—'

Elsa's hand gesture told her to stay put.

'I re-joined your mother inside the shelter,' she continued, taking no notice of her niece's interjection. 'She'd forgotten to pick up her air-raid bag before rushing out, but when there was a pause in the bombing I managed to run back and grab it. There were just a few items of clothing and some personal effects in it … Oh, and a biscuit tin housing some photos.'

Elsa paused again, trying to recall what happened next. I couldn't help wondering what she meant by 'personal effects'. The diary, perhaps? Did she hand Mum back the bag with all its contents?

'Were there any photos of my parents in the tin?'

'All I remember is that, many years later, she gifted me that biscuit tin containing photos of our BdM days. I've treasured them all my life. Would you like to see them?'

'Another time, perhaps, auntie,' Bettina said. 'You must be tired. And it's almost time for your supper.'

I was more than keen to see the photos, and to talk to Elsa about her experiences in the Hitler Youth. I wanted to quiz her about the time when Mum was looking after evacuated children in Lower Silesia; possibly even confront her with that incriminating photo of her, her husband and Dad in front of the Groß-Rosen camp. However, I didn't want to burn my bridges with Bettina. To find out the truth, and the diary's whereabouts, I needed her as an ally.

'Perhaps another time,' I bit my lip, reluctantly agreeing with Bettina. 'I don't wish to outstay my welcome, but I'd really like to come back and look at your photos. You might like to see some of my mother's pictures from that era, as well.'

'That would be very nice.' Bettina pre-empted her aunt's reply with a polite cliché. Was that faint smile around the corner of her lips a gesture of gratitude, or did I imagine it?

Weeks went by without any further contact. Had I been too keen, and frightened them off? Had the niece made the connection between my family and my research interests? Elsa clearly hadn't. She had been much more forthcoming than I had expected, but Bettina appeared to keep a tight rein on her. How much did she know about Elsa's past? Was she scared of me asking what her aunt was really up to in 1944? Would she even know about the Groß-Rosen camp? I needed to talk to her in private and allay her fears so that she would allow me to meet with Elsa again.

Elsa's impromptu narrative bore similarities with that of Mrs Rau, the eyewitness I'd interviewed in the Vivat home. Both accounts dealt with coming under attack from Allied bombings, and were remembered particularly clearly, since they happened on their eighteenth and twenty-first birthdays respectively. They also fitted neatly into our book's classification system under category one, 'Victimisation – "we lost everything and suffered just as much"'. As yet, however, we hadn't found any narratives to exemplify the fifth category, 'Being fascinated – "there were also good times"' category. But there was a good chance that this was still to come.

My academic work had always come first, but during the last few weeks I had neglected it badly. Unmarked essays were piling up on my desk, unanswered correspondence lay in my in-tray and there were pages of ignored emails. I had missed appointments, and students complained about tutorials that had been cancelled at short notice. I'd been too preoccupied with my family research, gradually slipping out of the normal role that I had long since assigned myself: the detached historian, the neutral arbiter who could look at primary sources without bias or emotion.

Now I needed to stop chasing the dragons of my youth, seeking answers to questions I had been scared to ask my entire life. I urgently needed to get back to work and catch up. But how could I abandon my quest for the truth? I was so close to unravelling some of the strands of my parents' history. And in the process I had even met up with Elsa, an eyewitness personally involved in the Holocaust.

Two days of solid essay marking, but my mind was elsewhere. What excuse could I use to get in touch with Bettina? The next day I called her on the pretext of needing information about the children's evacuation scheme during the war. I asked her if she could locate any source material for me in the British Library. I had come across another innocent-sounding Nazi euphemism for evacuation: *Kinderlandverschickung* – the relocation of children to the countryside. Many years after the war, the term was still used to refer to the tradition of sending sick and underprivileged children on heavily subsidised holidays. I can vouch for that, since my mother thought it would be a cheap and enjoyable holiday for her ten-year old son. I hated every minute, every second, of it.

Bettina called a week later, inviting me to the library to show me what she'd managed to locate.

'Thank you so much for your help. Very kind, and exceedingly useful,' I said as we sat down for lunch in the library's café. 'I also wanted to apologise if I outstayed my welcome when I visited a few weeks ago. Was there a reason you didn't like your aunt telling me about—?'

'No, it's just … She can get very agitated when talking about the war. I know that the eyewitness accounts are important for your book, but—'

'I do understand. My mother did, as well, when I asked her to open up about her experiences. But don't you think those eyewitness accounts are vital for the next generations – to allow them to grasp what was going on at the time; to understand why their parents or grandparents behaved the way they did.'

Her face showed little sign of approval or agreement.

'How is your aunt, by the way. Is she OK?' I continued.

'She's alright now. Much better than last year. I had to move her out of the Vivat home. The press can be quite cruel.'

'How do you mean?'

'Don't you know? They hounded her out of the home, because her husband was an SS officer during the war. It all started when *Days of Fear* was published.'

'I'm so sorry. I had no idea. I shouldn't have brought the book along. Has she talked to you about her husband at all?'

I took a large bite out of my sandwich and started chewing. Should I tell her the truth? That Herbert Kohl was hanged at the Nuremberg trials for mass murder? That her aunt had worked as a concentration camp guard? How much did Bettina really know? And what would knowing anything *achieve*? It could scupper my chances of speaking to Elsa again; maybe derail everything I'd been working so hard for.

'She talked briefly about him once, when I asked her,' Bettina continued. 'Her husband rang her late one night urging her to pack immediately. I guess this must have been towards the end of the war. "The Russians are breaking through our defences," he had warned her. He promised to pick her up in his Jeep that night. I think she also mentioned that they were both at the Eastern Front, but I'm not entirely certain. Anyway, he never turned up and she thinks he was killed in action. She doesn't really want to talk about it any more, and I respect that.'

Bettina got up and filled her glass from the water dispenser.

'Look,' she said eventually, having taken a deep breath, 'I know your mother and Elsa were good friends, but I barely know you. I know you're researching a book, but what's the point of stirring up the past and upsetting people?'

Not again! 'Stirring up the past' – that phrase was so reminiscent of Helmut's sentiments: 'Sometimes it's good to leave the past *in* the past.' Was I about to fight a similar battle with Bettina?

'I'm sorry. I didn't mean to pry. Your aunt and my mother were both active members in the BdM, you see, and the Hitler Youth forms part of our research for the book. Do you think your aunt would mind talking to me about this? Would it upset her?'

'On the contrary. She loves talking about the BdM. She thinks it was the best time of her life – which I find somewhat disturbing.'

'Quite. And that's why it's so fascinating to hear from eyewitnesses, so we can try to understand how so many young people got sucked into this organisation.'

'Do I sense a bit of a personal agenda in the historian's research here?'

'Of course.'

'To be candid with you, I think you'll find that my aunt isn't exactly a reformed character.'

'I'm sure I can slip back into the role of detached historian, and I promise not to argue with her. When would it be convenient for me to visit again?'

'You don't lose much time, do you! Under one condition: under no circumstance is my aunt to be named as an eyewitness in your book.'

'Agreed. As a matter of fact, all of our eyewitnesses have fictional names, to protect their identity.'

As she was about to leave, she added, 'By the way, are any of your students looking for somewhere to live? We're renting out a couple of rooms on the second floor. We need the money.'

I promised I'd look into it and let her know.

I punched the air on my way to uni. Somehow, I had

managed to wriggle my way back into Elsa's citadel and would be able to chat with her about the BdM, share old photos with her and sneak in the Groß-Rosen photograph. But how would she react?

Sam was very pleased to hear my news, but still queried me about the longer-term strategy. I had none.

'What do you suggest, then?' I asked.

'Woo her. The niece, I mean. Buy her flowers, take her out, spend some time with her. She will confide in you – eventually. She might know if Elsa has your mum's diary and could confirm details of Elsa's work in the camp.'

'I want to find out what she knows, but not like that. She seems quite genuine. Her aunt obviously hasn't told her the truth about Herbert Kohl. She invented some story: "He died fighting the Russians."'

'She can't be that naive, surely. I'd be on my guard if I were you. Good luck, anyway! And don't forget next Tuesday: we need to try and finalise the last three chapters.'

'I know. I'll be there, no worries. Ooh, and before I forget: are any of your students still looking for digs?'

'Why?'

'Bettina said they're going to let a couple of rooms.'

'What?' He stared at me, his eyes wide, mouth half open. 'You lucky, lucky devil.'

'How so? Oh, I see. You mean me moving—?'

'God, you're slow. This is your big chance to move in and find out the truth. I'm sure you can conjure up some spurious reason why you need temporary accommodation.'

I told him I'd think about it and left it at that.

At home, I dipped into Mum's shoebox again – the one with the old photographs. I selected a few pictures of her in her BdM leader's uniform, marching in step with her girls through the woods, supervising sports competitions and directing the youth choir. I felt they would help to jog Elsa's memory, and nicely complement the photographs she wanted to show *me*. As preparation for my next visit, I also re-read Mum's memoirs, *My Childhood and Youth in the League of German Girls of the Hitler Youth*. I was dismayed to read in the introduction that occasionally she still felt that she was betraying an ideology she had committed herself to, by an oath of allegiance in the BdM. Although the memoirs were meant to critically evaluate her time in the BdM, long passages of the book were an almost glowing tribute to her girls for their achievements in sports, arts and crafts, and to their overall discipline, obedience and camaraderie. Only later in the book did she become aware of the distinct imperialist message of most of the songs she sang with her girls. Consider this one:

Nach Ostland geht unser Ritt
Eastwards we are riding
hoch wehen die Banner im Winde,
with banners flying high in the wind,
die Rosse, sie traben geschwinde.
our horses are riding swiftly.
Auf, Brüder, die Kräfte gespannt,
Come on, brothers: muster all your strength,
wir reiten in neues Land.
for we are riding into the Promised Land.

Then there was a description of a typical day in the BdM summer camp, which bore an uncanny resemblance to my early 1960s experiences in the *Kinderlandverschickung* on the North Sea island of Norderney … although without the political indoctrination. Getting up at 6.00, early-morning exercise, cold shower, making beds – followed by an inspection – breakfast, singing, raising the flag, excursion into the woods or sports. After lunch, which was at 12.00, an hour of free time, followed by political education, including topics such as 'The Arian race, great leaders, our enemies'. Then more sports, arts and crafts sessions and singing, dinner at 6.00, dormitory, lights out at 9.00. Oh, I almost forgot: there was a rota for every imaginable chore – setting and clearing the table, stacking chairs, washing up, cleaning, laundry service, wiping our leaders' …Well, *almost* every chore!

I wondered how much of this ideology, with its deeply ingrained norms and values, was carried over into post-war German society. Order, discipline, obedience – the regimented society. I hated every minute of my 'holiday' in the *Kinderlandverschickung*. 'May I read my book now?' I'd once asked one of the leaders.

Later on in the evening, I took the conch shell out from my cigar box and stamped hard on it. I wanted no more reminders of my North Sea island holiday.

'BdM? The best time of my life,' Elsa had said, apparently. What was there to rave about, Elsa?

I would soon find out.

Chapter 13

A sea of snowdrops – nodding white flowers with just a dab of green – lined the footpath to The Doctor's House. Although this sight would normally have lifted my spirits, my mind was still in a state of disarray. Here I was again, about to talk to yet another eyewitness who believed that their life had been determined by forces over which they had little or no control. While previous interviewees had either focused on the 'victim's' perspective or framed their narrative conveniently as 'the best we could do under the circumstances', here was one who was complicit in the murderous regime – and seemingly unrepentant, at that.

What was even more bizarre was that the lines of our research for *Fractured Lives* had unwittingly crossed over into my own family history, its threads twisted into an intricate knot that was proving difficult to untangle. Mother and Elsa had been comrades in the BdM, both displaying a youthful enthusiasm for the Third Reich. Dad had also been friendly with Elsa, but *how* friendly? Did either of my parents know about her work at Groß-Rosen? Would the diary provide any answers?

Elsa was sitting exactly where I had seen her on my first visit – in the same position, almost motionless. Had it not been for the occasional puffs of smoke emanating from her meerschaum pipe, I could easily have believed she'd just died in her chair. A silver tin with *XOX Keks* engraved on the lid sat next to her on the coffee table.

'Jonas! Sit next to me.' Her perfume smelled floral and overly powdery, not unlike baby powder mixed with lavender. Bettina had positioned herself in her usual place on the sofa, and was casting a watchful eye from a distance.

There it was – the darkest chapter in German history captured in snapshots housed in a biscuit tin. A whole spectrum of photographs ranging from proud soldiers celebrating Wehrmacht victories to images of destroyed cities and the defeated struggling for survival in the rubble. And, of course, many BdM snaps – all square, black-and-white photographs measuring 4.5 centimetres, on chamois paper, straight-edged, no *Büttenrand*.

Elsa put down her pipe and started rummaging around in the tin with both hands, moving the ones from the bottom to the top. She seemed to have found what she was looking for. Gathering a small number of photographs in one hand like a pack of cards, she dealt them out one by one.

'You can take notes for your book, if you want to. Some of these have a story to tell.' She handed me the first photo.

'There's your mother with our girls! And that's me, the standard-bearer ... There, right behind her ... Look!' she said proudly, pointing at a tall young woman in plaits. 'I was second in command.'

There they were: Mother and Elsa, leading a group of about thirty ten- to twelve-year-olds on a hike through the forest. It was almost an exact copy of the photograph I'd brought along – the girls marching in twos, white blouses over long black skirts, each sporting a neckerchief held in place by a leather woggle.

'Snap!' I said, taking out one of Mum's photographs.

Elsa smiled – a rare occurrence.

'We had such a good time …' She passed me a few more snaps from her deck: girls sitting around the campfire, all in uniform, singing and playing the guitar; another group of girls in white sport dresses, gracefully throwing balls up in the air, all in perfect synchrony.

'Our girls were pretty good at gymnastics – and, of course, track and field sports,' she said, nodding like one of those toy dogs you see in the back of cars.

'Any photos of BdM social gatherings? Mother used to called them *home evenings*.'

Elsa rummaged around in her tin, but couldn't find any.

'Aah, the *Heimabende* … Yes, they were good fun, too. And very educational. We taught the girls about healthy living and hygiene, and trained them up for their future roles in society as good wives, mothers and homemakers.'

I was itching to respond, but Bettina gave me a stern look, shaking her head in a fashion that clearly said: 'Don't.' So I kept my thoughts to myself. The BdM girls of those days – mothers-in-waiting – had to be healthy in order to produce lots of children for the Führer. No makeup, no smoking, cleanliness, discipline and order. Campfire romanticism, sports and 'education' were all used to indoctrinate impressionable young girls and boys with the National Socialist ideology. 'He alone who owns the youth gains the future' was one of Hitler's phrases.

I leaned over the open biscuit tin and took another peek.

'Who's this?' I asked, pointing to a portrait of a teenager in rags. Elsa looked puzzled, took a magnifying glass from the coffee table and read the small pencil marks on the back: *Joshua, March 1945.*

'Oh, I remember Joshua. The little Jew boy from Poland. He came to us one night, begging for food. Mind you, he didn't look like a Jew. Well, not like the ones on posters or in the *Wochenschau* we were familiar with. He had black hair, pleasant features and blue eyes, but his clothes were in tatters. He was as thin as a rake.'

'What had happened to him?' I asked.

'He was terrified to the bone. He'd been hiding in the woods for months – the whole family had. When he appeared on our doorstep, he put his hands up, saying, "I'm a Jew! The Russians have killed my family, all of them." Apparently, the family had told the Russians that they weren't German, but it didn't make any difference. He sobbed long and deep. Then he told us about his escape, fleeing from one hiding place to another, only venturing out at night.'

'Did you help him?'

'We didn't know what to do with him. We, too, were fleeing from the Eastern Front. Helping a Jew – even not reporting one – was dangerous. However, we did give him food and drink.'

'What happened then?'

'Obviously, we couldn't take him with us, but we showed him a cubbyhole outside our barracks. He crawled into it on all fours … and that's the last I saw of him.'

She turned away from me, relit her pipe, and added: 'You see, the Russians didn't like the Jews either. And the Poles helped German soldiers to find Jews wherever they were hiding, then entered their houses and began to plunder as soon as they were taken away. Some even robbed the

Jewish corpses when the shooting was over.'

An awkward silence followed. I covered my face with my hands, bowing my head. I found Elsa's nonchalant attitude towards her story hard to stomach, but I'd promised Bettina not to challenge or upset her aunt.

'Anyone for tea or coffee?' Bettina broke the embarrassing silence.

'My usual, Tina.'

'And – for you? Coffee, white, no sugar?' She didn't wait for an answer, and disappeared into the kitchen.

'Your mother was in great danger once.' Elsa continued the conversation unperturbed. 'Amongst her group of evacuated children, she had a half-Jewish girl. She didn't report her to the authorities as she should have done. She could have gone to prison for that.'

'That was very brave of her. Was that near Liegnitz, in the children's evacuation home? I think I have a photograph taken near there.'

Would this be an opportune moment to confront her with the photograph – the one of her, her husband and Dad in front of the Groß-Rosen camp? She seemed to have no problem remembering events with an emotional content, like her eighteenth birthday, when they had to rush into the air-raid shelter. Also, the whole picture gallery of her 'enjoyable' time in the BdM had been securely stored in the dark cellars of her mind. But would the Groß-Rosen photograph trigger any memories?

'This must be your husband,' I said innocently, handing her the photograph. Her face suddenly began to twitch nervously, as though a small creature had been confined beneath her skin and was struggling violently to escape.

She handed the photo back without comment, then rose slowly from her armchair, pipe still clenched between her teeth. 'Excuse me. I must spend a penny.'

When she walked past, she lingered for a moment, then looked down on me. I suddenly froze – feeling the prison guard's gaze boring through me, it was as if I was about to be assessed. 'Fit for work, labour camp three. Take him away!' I looked up at her face. Her lips hadn't moved. She was still sending little puffs of smoke up into the cold air.

As she left the room, Bettina came back in, and put the drinks tray down on the coffee table.

'I feel the photograph you just showed my aunt has upset her somewhat. May I see it, please?'

I tried to read Bettina's face as I handed it over, feeling like a recalcitrant schoolboy. Did she also recognise the location, and its significance?

'I told you before: she doesn't want to be reminded of her husband. It upsets her deeply. Why did you bring this photograph?' she snarled.

'I'm sorry. I meant no harm. I merely wanted to know if she'd recognise my dad. Here – the one on the right. Also, whether they'd been good friends.'

'That's a feeble excuse,' she said, half-sententiously. Then, out of the blue, added, 'Can we stop playing this charade! You and I know *very well* where this photograph was taken. And you most likely also know what really happened to her husband.'

'You told me he was killed in action.'

'That was the story my aunt told me. But anybody who knows about the Nuremberg trials – especially historians like you – knows the truth.'

'So, why—?'

'Because I was playing you at your own game. Elsa doesn't know that I know. And you must never ever tell her. I just want her to live out the rest of her life in peace and quiet. She's suffered enough, don't you think? First her uncle dying in the firestorm in Cologne, and then her husband at the trials. What's the point in opening up old wounds?'

We faced each other in silence for a moment. I stared at her transfixed, racking my brains, not knowing how to respond.

'What do you really want from us, Jonas?'

'OK. No more charades. I'll be honest with you. I want to find out as much as I can about my parents' role in the war. Your aunt is the last survivor who knew them both, so I thought looking at old photographs would help to jog her memory. I'd like to discover what she knew about my dad, whether there is any correspondence between her and my mother, or if any other documents exist from that time.'

'I can't help you there. She's a very private person – she keeps her cards close to her chest, always locks her study. I was surprised to hear the story about the Jewish boy. She's never mentioned him before.'

She paused briefly to pour the tea and coffee.

'So the eyewitness stories are just a convenient by-product for your book, are they?'

'No, not at all. They form an essential part. Biography and contemporary history are interwoven in a complex way and we're recording the war experiences of our eyewitnesses for posterity. They're a slowly dying generation, whose stories will fill a gap in contemporary history books. By some curious coincidence, the eyewitness trail eventually led to your aunt, as well.'

'I see.'

'I'm really sorry. I didn't mean to upset her. It's just that … My mum's recent death means I've lost the most important eyewitness for my own family research.'

The bathroom door slammed shut, announcing Elsa's imminent return.

A quick conversation change. 'Oh, by the way, Bettina. I've got some news for you, about the rooms you want to let.'

'Good. Have you found us a lodger?'

'Well, I've just accepted an offer on my flat, but the house I'm buying is not quite ready for me to move into, so I was wondering—'

'You'll have to ask my aunt.' Bettina cut me short. Did I detect some disapproval in her voice? She placed the lid firmly back on the tin that housed Elsa's photos.

'Ask me what?' Elsa croaked, shuffling back into the lounge.

Once she'd settled back in her armchair, I said loudly, 'I also came to ask you a favour.'

'I'm an old woman, but I hear very well. What do you want?'

'Well, I've sold my flat and put an offer in on a new house, which will take some time … I'm looking for somewhere to live in the meantime. I wondered—'

'You'd have to pay rent,' she said, with unexpected rudeness.

'Of course. I wouldn't expect you to put me up for free!'

'He could have the two empty rooms on the first floor,' Bettina piped up. I knew from our discussion in the library that she'd wanted to let the rooms to students, to generate some additional income for her impoverished aunt. However, I was taken aback by her readiness to accept *me* as a lodger.

'Two rooms – six hundred pounds a month, paid in advance,' Elsa continued.

'That's absolutely fine. Thank you so much.'

Three weeks later, I moved in.

They say that you don't really get to know a person until you live in the same house. I got to know the house fairly well, but not its inhabitants – at least, not for a while. Both women kept themselves to themselves. They kept their distance, and their doors firmly shut. It was as though they barely noticed my existence.

Elsa occupied a suite of rooms on the ground floor, next to the old scullery. Bettina owned two rooms on the first floor, plus her own bathroom. Her bedroom was adjacent to Elsa's study, which – unless she was working in there – was always kept locked. My rooms were at the opposite end of a long corridor, a safe distance from Bettina's rooms. To avoid ever going past their living quarters, I was instructed to use a separate staircase that led down into the hall near the front door.

Apart from a sturdy double bed, every single piece of furniture in my rooms looked as if it had fallen off the back of a lorry on its way to a charity shop. Even the shower cubicle in my bedroom was an ill-conceived afterthought. To be fair, by prior arrangement I *was* allowed to take a bath in Bettina's bathroom – which proved to be an interesting experience, when one evening I decided to take her up on her kind offer, out of sheer curiosity.

I often wondered what exactly it is that gives a room a male or female touch. The bathroom definitely read feminine to me, thanks to soft colours, floral prints on the blind and matching fabric on the three-legged stool. Scented candles, a loofah sponge and a packet of fizzy bath bombs containing 'natural essential oils' sat on the side of the bath. Needless to say, I brought my own body wash and shampoo.

I couldn't resist taking a peek in her bathroom cabinet, however. The top shelf was crammed full of nail varnishes of every possible colour and, underneath, some cotton wool, nail varnish remover and various chemicals to remove unwanted body hair. The medicine shelf at the bottom housed antihistamines, nasal spray and some suspicious holistic treatments, as well as an array of painkillers.

Was sharing Bettina's bathroom the closest I would ever get to her? And what lay behind Elsa's locked study door? I'd taken Sam's advice to take up residence in their house, but I started to wonder whether this costly experiment would ever bear fruit.

Elsa and Bettina lived their strange isolated existence in The Doctor's House, and went through their daily routines – of which I knew very little. That is, until …

One evening I heard a strange, mechanical noise at the other end of the corridor. It sounded like the clatter of an old-fashioned electric typewriter, and every so often there'd be a ping at the end of the line. Normally, the house would be dead quiet by 9.30. I took off my shoes and went to explore. It was pitch dark, except for a dim light shining through from underneath the door of Elsa's study. I slid quietly over the threshold of my room and began to creep towards hers, guided only by the line of the banister under my searching hand. I could hear Elsa talking in a low voice. Now and then, Bettina would interrupt, as though asking for clarification. As I eased slowly forward, I felt the creaky floorboards give beneath my socks. I hesitated, wondering whether to continue. Then I heard Elsa's voice again, cool and low, sounding somewhat desperate. I could distinguish the word 'Tina' and, later, 'I implore you.'

My next step was more audible than I'd expected. The floorboard groaned as if I had stepped on someone's toe. I stopped, listened intently, stifling my own breath for a moment. There was a different sound now – footsteps in Elsa's study. Suddenly the door opened. I turned and ran for cover towards my room. I closed the door behind me and stood still, no breathing. I heard Bettina's quizzical voice.

'Anyone there?'

Shortly afterwards, the typewriter fell silent.

The next morning, Bettina knocked at my door. I'd just come out of the shower and was still in my bathrobe. Was she going to accuse me about last night's eavesdropping? I was convinced she hadn't seen me, though. I opened the door very slightly.

'Sorry to disturb you, but I'm taking my aunt to the doctor's. She's been unwell for a few days now. Would you mind looking in on her when we're back? I have to go into work this afternoon.'

'Yes, of course. It's my research day today, so I can easily work from home.'

Bettina seemed relieved. She later confided in me that her aunt would often sit still for hours, musing and dozing, and that she was sometimes so motionless she feared Elsa was dead.

Shortly afterwards, they left. I was alone in the house for the very first time, away from prying eyes … and desperate to unearth what lay behind Elsa's locked study door. Although I knew it would be useless, I still tried the door handle. Locked. Her study was on the first floor with a double-aspect window on the west wing.

If the window cleaner could get up there, then so could I. It didn't take me long to locate a ladder in the garden shed. To extend it to its full height, there were a couple of hinges that needed unlocking. The rungs seemed quite far apart, so I had to hold on with both hands not to miss a step. I'm terrible with heights, so I didn't dare look down. I finally reached the windowsill of Elsa's study. One more step, and I'd be able to peer in.

The room was divided into two alcoves by a pair of chest-high bookcases. By the window stood a small desk with a chair tucked underneath, its surface cluttered with papers and mementos. An old-fashioned electric typewriter sat in the middle, its cable detached alongside it. On top of the typewriter rested an open booklet in a strange format – somewhere between A5 and A4 – which showed neat handwriting on yellowed, lined paper. I screwed my eyes up to try and decipher what was on the page. Some words and phrases seemed to be crossed out with a red pen, and corrected versions written on top or in the margins. The narrow edges of the booklet revealed a brown leather cover, worn and torn in places. I couldn't read any of the writing from where I stood, but it looked like there might be a date in the top right-hand corner of the page.

Surely this couldn't be Mum's diary. She would never have rewritten her own diary, corrections still visible.

Beneath the other window stood a chaise longue and a nest of tables with a small picture frame on it. I stared at the image in utter disbelief. Oh my God! It was a portrait of Dad and Elsa – both of them in uniform, arm in arm, and happily smiling into the camera. I tightened my grip on the ladder. As I slowly descended, my knees felt like jelly.

Bettina dropped Elsa off around lunchtime, then left for work. I was determined to discover the truth about Elsa and Dad's relationship, and at some stage I promised myself I would ask Bettina about the strange nightly typing sessions. With Bettina away at work for the afternoon, I took my chance to confront Elsa and knocked at her living room door.

'Are you OK? Bettina told me you've been to see the doctor.'

'Yes, he thinks it's bronchitis, but I think it's just a bit of a cough. Nothing to worry about.'

'Well, I do hope it's nothing serious. By the way, I've brought a few more photos to show you.' She gave me a quizzical glance. I smiled at her reassuringly and opened up the photo wallet.

'Look. That's you and Mum there. You were quite a bit taller than her, weren't you? And there's one of the three of you, with Dad sitting in the middle. Lucky man!'

None of them are wearing uniform. Dad, with his rolled-up sleeves, is sitting on the ground between them, and has a self-satisfied smirk on his face. Mum is smiling a little shyly into the camera. Both she and Elsa are perched on a wooden bench behind him. Mum is leaning slightly forward, resting her right hand on his shoulder, while Elsa sits upright with a somewhat artificial smile.

Elsa sat up in her armchair and readjusted her glasses. She pointed to a slight bulge in Mum's dress and checked the pencilled date on the back of the photograph: *1 May 1944*.

'Your mother was pregnant then. She married Rudi two months later in July. She was the lucky one.'

'How do you mean?'

'Your father and I were going out when the war started. He was my first love. We lost touch when he was stationed in Crete and later in the Balkans. By the time his regiment was moved to Liegnitz, he'd already met Cäcilia. And that was that.' She gazed pensively at the picture, then added, 'I married my old school friend, Herbert, two months later, on 8 September 1944.'

Remembering that day, a smile began to soften Elsa's sombre face. But why did the date ring a bell for me? Of course … It was the day the first V-2 rocket landed in London. I checked the facts. Launched from a mobile unit, the lethal rocket carried a ton of explosives. Luckily the first one killed only three people. 'V' stood for *Vergeltungswaffen* (retaliation weapons) – Hitler's last-ditch attempt to reverse the course of the war. More than 1,300 V-2s were launched during the last year of the war, causing large-scale devastation and huge loss of life amongst the civilian population. I wondered whether that news would have reached Elsa and her husband on their wedding day.

Although Elsa had partially satisfied my curiosity about her relationship with my father, it had inadvertently opened up a whole litany of further questions. How well did Dad know Herbert? Did he know that Elsa's husband had been in charge of a concentration camp? Had Elsa been working in the same camp? She'd already lied to Bettina about her husband's death, so there was no point confronting her about it. Besides, I'd promised Bettina not to upset her aunt.

I was tempted to dig deeper – to ask Elsa what happened to her at the end of the war – when I heard the key turn in the front-door lock. I quickly gathered up the photographs and hid them in my jacket.

'Can I get you anything, Mrs Roberts? Or would you like to wait? I think Bettina's just come back.'

Bettina marched in, throwing her coat and bag on the sofa.

'Hi, Auntie.' She acknowledged me with a mere nod of the head. 'Nice of Jonas to look in on you, isn't it? Did you have a nice chat? How are you feeling?'

'There's nothing wrong with me, you know. And I will carry on smoking, despite what the doctor said.'

Bettina sighed, and took me to one side. 'The doctor said she's got chronic obstructive pulmonary disease, most likely caused by her smoking. I'm exceedingly worried about her.'

'Look, do you want to get her supper first? We can talk in my room after that.'

An hour later, she knocked at my door. She was still wearing her work outfit, a knee-length maroon dress with a modest V-neck and some clever ruching around the waist.

'I can't get her to give up smoking. I've tried everything. She's so bloody stubborn … and so contrary. One day, she tells me she hasn't got long to live and wants to finish writing her memoirs; the next day, she says there's nothing wrong with her. You just heard her.'

'It can't be easy for you – working part-time and pretty much being her full-time carer. Wouldn't she qualify for NHS home care?'

'She hates people coming into the house. I think she still suffers from some kind of persecution complex. She jumps every time the doorbell rings. We have no social life, Jonas – no visitors, no friends. I don't know how the days pass. I rarely go out with work colleagues, and when I do, I feel guilty. I don't think I can go on like this much longer.'

I was touched by her openness, her sincerity. Like a compass needle changing direction, her mind had rapidly repositioned itself from reclusive to candid.

We sat down facing each other. Moving my chair closer to hers, I said: 'You need some respite. You have to get out of the house sometimes. I'm going to a guitar concert next Saturday. Come with me – I can get you a ticket.'

'I'd love that. And thank you for listening. It means a lot to me.'

Chapter 14

University life reasserted its familiar routine – teaching, marking, meetings and, wherever possible, carving out time for research. At the end of each spring term, the History department traditionally organised a panel discussion – open to any interested staff and students – on a general interest topic. This time it was Sam's and my turn to chair the discussion. Our notice on the board read:

HISTORY FROM THE BOTTOM–UP
What exactly does ordinary people's history add to
traditional historiography?
17 March, 11.00–12.00
Lecture Theatre L1
All welcome.

I sat in my office writing the introduction. Sam and I had often led heated discussions about the value and reliability of eyewitness accounts. We had rehearsed all the major counter-arguments to our bottom-up approach that the panel discussion – and, once published, the critics of *Fractured Lives* – could throw at us. The lapse of eyewitness memory, the inaccuracy of their remembered past and the subjective spin they'd put on their narratives – all in order to appear in a better light. Not to mention whether our method of selection would yield some meaningful patterns in their narratives, from which we could draw some general conclusions. Defending our approach, we would point out…

I hadn't typed anything for a few minutes when the screensaver started to obscure my notes. I glanced across the room to the door, noticing that I'd hung up my jacket in a hurry – the wrong way round. On the inside pocket, a photo wallet stuck out. It contained the photographs I had shown Elsa a couple of days ago. I couldn't resist looking at them again, and felt a strange sensation being dragged back to my chat with Elsa, imagining what she must have felt as she'd stared at the Groß-Rosen picture from spring 1944. Had she already decided to marry Herbert by then? Or was she still hankering after Dad - her first love? Did she not wish to comment, fearing she'd give away vital information about her workplace? Clever Bettina didn't need to be prompted about the location, but did she also know about her aunt working in a concentration camp? If so, would she still try to protect her from extradition?

I also wondered whether the smiling faces in the photographs had any inkling of Germany's impending defeat – the Allied landing in Normandy in June, the first Russian troops reaching Poland in July 1944. Would they have listened to banned British or French radio broadcasts? Even if they didn't, I'm sure Dad, working in counter-espionage, would have had some awareness of what was really going on. Maybe that's why my parents made their will on 20 September 1944, a mere two months after their wedding.

'You still OK writing the introduction for the panel discussion?' Sam asked as he came into my office. He saw me perusing the photographs. 'Has the inmate made any new discoveries? And how's the relationship-building going?'

'Sorry. Yes, fine. Got a bit distracted.'

'And?'

'Elsa told me she had a relationship with Dad before he met my mother. It turns out that she and my mum shared more than just BdM experiences. I didn't even have to prompt her. Herbert was only second choice.'

'And a bad one, at that. Did she admit working at Groß-Rosen? And what about the diary?'

'No, but she was visibly shaken – twitching all over when I showed her the photo. No trace of the diary, though. Although I have a feeling Bettina is helping her aunt to type up her memoirs. It's all a bit hush-hush, but I heard typing noises the other night.'

'Maybe she's writing about the camp's murderous regime, to get it off her chest. Then we'd have definite proof of her involvement.'

'No chance. She wouldn't let me read it and I can't get into her study. I tried. It's always locked.'

'Can't the niece get hold of the manuscript? We'd probably only need to copy a few pages.'

'Maybe she'll help. She's been a lot more amenable recently. Plus, I'm taking her out on Saturday.'

'Progress, indeed! That's good. By the way, I Googled "The Doctor's House" the other day. You won't believe it, but the infamous Dr Wright used to live there. If you remember, he murdered fifteen of his patients – mostly elderly women. He was convicted twelve years ago, but committed suicide in prison. Macabre news, eh?'

'Thanks for that. You really know how to cheer a man up.'

I stayed the night at *my* house and finished writing the introduction.

Saturday beckoned. As agreed, at 6.30 I went to pick Bettina up. Her bedroom door had been left ajar. Inside, she stood in front of a long mirror, alternately hoisting her black velvet dress up and letting it down again, frowning critically. She seemed to have a serious problem, and couldn't decide whether or not her dress, which sat just short of her knees, was too long. Did she, for a wild moment, wish she had *shortened* it? Hearing my footsteps, she pushed the door wide open.

'I'm almost ready. Come in,' she mumbled as she put the finishing touches of red lipstick to her half-open mouth.

Her dress was almost backless, revealing her perfect white skin, and made of the kind of soft fabric you almost can't resist touching. I thought it suited her remarkably well and took years off her age. She certainly didn't look like a woman in her early forties.

'Lovely dress,' I said, with real conviction.

'Thank you.' She turned round to pick up her clutch bag. 'I don't think I've ever been to a classical guitar concert.' There was a touch of embarrassment in her voice. 'But I do like listening to guitar music. Do you play?'

'I used to, but haven't played for quite a while. It's a really varied programme. There are a few famous Baroque pieces in the first half, followed in the second by contemporary composers like Leo Brouwer and Hans Werner Henze. But there's also a piece you might recognise.'

We arrived at the concert hall in time for a glass of wine at its overcrowded bar.

'This is nice,' she said, raising her glass for a toast. 'I

haven't been out for ages.'

'Me, neither. It's not much fun going out on your own.'

We left it there. No intrusive follow-up questions about relationships – past or current. Bettina simply changed the subject.

'So, how's the house purchase progressing?'

'A few more weeks, I reckon. Then you'll be rid of me.'

'I didn't mean it like that.'

'How did you find The Doctor's House? It must have needed quite a bit of work before you could move in.'

'It still does. My aunt found it. It'd been on the market for quite a while, so she got it for a bargain price. It still used up all her savings, though. At the time, I was living with my English boyfriend in a tiny one-bedroom flat in South London. I like having all the space, though it gets a bit spooky at times. It would be interesting to explore the house's history, but I'm not sure I'll ever find the time. My aunt can be very demanding, you know.'

'You seem to be very devoted to her – and very patient.'

'She looked after me when my parents died in a car accident. I was only ten. So I owe her, don't you think?'

Ushers were passing through the crowded foyer, urging people to take their seats in the concert hall. We returned our empty glasses to the bar and joined the slow-moving queue.

'There's a piece in the second half I think I recognise,' Bettina whispered, pointing at 'Cavatina' in the programme. 'Isn't that the theme from *The Deer Hunter*?'

'Yes, you're right. It's a lovely piece, but not easy to play. This first piece here – Bach's Chaconne in D minor – is my favourite.'

As the guitarist came on stage, enthusiastic applause stifled the cacophony of voices. It took a few more minutes for the music to start: tuning, listening again, adjusting the strings slightly, then playing a few arpeggio chords to check the tuning. Then, all of a sudden, the majestic sequence of dissonant chords of the opening phrase seized – and held – our attention. Phrase upon phrase built up, the tension increasing with a dexterity of flourishes and melodic inventions held us in thrall. It's emotionally so powerful and structurally perfect, with its concluding fugal movement. I was utterly mesmerised. I felt as though I had been dragged through a rollercoaster of emotions that had left me breathless.

The back of my hand, I noticed, had brushed against Bettina's, then casually rested there on the armrest, next to hers. She didn't move her hand away. Did that mean she didn't mind? I took the risk: my fingers closed over hers. I felt a responsive pressure and, looking up, saw that she was smiling at me.

In the interval we talked about the power of music, how it can invite reflection, awaken feelings, activate memories, touch the heart. I wasn't sure whether the second half of the programme with its modern pieces would appeal to Bettina in the same way, but she loved the cavatina. The concert had seemingly been acting as a bond between us, touching both of us in our own unique way.

In the wine bar afterwards, the conversation took on a more intimate tone.

'Are you seeing anyone at the moment?' I asked blatantly.

'No. I split up with my boyfriend eighteen months ago.

A few months after that, he married a twenty-five-year-old, and now they're expecting a baby. He always told me he never wanted children.'

She took a big swig of red wine from the glass I had placed in front of her.

'Just not with *me*, clearly. He rang me last month to wish me happy birthday. Said he was grateful I hadn't made a fuss when we split. No drama, no violent scenes. He'd let me down gently, told me it would be best for both of us. I hated the pussyfooting around; his slimy tone of voice. I just wanted to throw something at him – preferably something heavy and breakable. He made me feel sick, so I hung up.'

I moved a little closer to Bettina, away from the woman standing next to me, who I thought was listening in to our conversation. 'Breaking up is never easy. Lucy, my wife, left me when our son, Ludger, was only eleven. She, also, remarried shortly afterwards. I had to go to court to arrange child custody. She'd poisoned our relationship by telling Ludger that the breakup was all his daddy's fault. When my mother died last year, she didn't even turn up at the funeral.'

'I'm sorry. I shouldn't have started on this. Especially after such a pleasant evening. Thank you for taking me. It was really lovely. Cheers!'

We returned home late, and a little intoxicated. As she opened the front door, I hesitated. For a moment I was about to say good night, to go back to my own house. I'd lied to them, saying the new house wasn't ready to move into, and just then I'd nearly given the game away. There *was* no new house.

'Aren't you coming in, Jonas? I haven't upset you, have I?'

'No, not at all. I was just—'

'Well, this is still your home for a few more weeks, until you move into your new house. Good night. And thanks again.' Stopping briefly at 'my' flight of stairs, she gave me a peck on the cheek, then disappeared into the dimly lit corridor.

I had a lie-in on Sunday, but awoke to the distant sound of the typewriter. It was the same clattering noise, with an occasional ping, that I'd heard before. I dressed double-quick, hurried down 'my' staircase, ran along the corridor, then halfway up the stairs leading to Bettina's room – where I could listen in on their conversation.

Elsa was talking in a croaky voice, coughing and spluttering intermittently. The typewriter rattled on, pinging at the end of each line. I caught snippets of her sentences: 'No, wait, that's all wrong, too.' And, later on, 'I need to rewrite this – again.'

Then the typewriter fell silent for a moment. I heard Bettina's stern voice. 'Just concentrate on what you want to say and stop drinking that disgusting Schnapps.' More coughing. Then Elsa continued with her dictation. I missed the bit at the beginning, but caught an entire sentence before the typewriter started up with its rattling: '… the Führer. I have believed in him ever since I was a child, and wanted to serve him for the rest of my life.'

I moved a few steps up the stairs. Dare I peek through the keyhole to get a glimpse of them? I waited until the typewriter noise started, to drown out any creaks from the floorboards. Two more steps towards the door. Kneeling down on my right knee, I rested my left hand on the other, ready to jump up and escape capture. My heart was beating twice as fast as normal. There she was: Elsa at her desk, and reading from the same booklet, in the strange format I'd seen before, when looking through her window from the outside. A lot of her neat handwriting had been crossed out with red pen, corrections scribbled on top and in much smaller writing in the margins. Of course, I couldn't make out any of the words from such a distance. In front of her, within easy reach, sat the white Schnapps bottle. A half-empty tumbler rested precariously on the desk's edge. The keyhole's narrow angle prevented me from seeing Bettina or the typewriter, however.

All of a sudden, there was a sound of shattering glass. I jumped up and scuttled swiftly along the corridor. Bettina let out a loud screech, then started shouting at her aunt.

'Look what you've done now. If you don't stop drinking and smoking, I won't help you.'

In the afternoon I sat in the neglected garden enjoying the early spring sunshine, occasionally glancing over the top of my book at my landlords' closed windows. There was no sign of life. Some of the shutters were still closed; others had their curtains half drawn. Bettina and her aunt passed their days in semi-darkness, as though they feared people might catch a glimpse of them – which only made me more suspicious that they had something to conceal. Did Elsa's memoirs contain incriminating material about her that Bettina needed to hide from me? Perhaps Sam was right: she was writing about her time as a Groß-Rosen guard to assuage her guilt. How could I persuade Bettina to let me into the shrine? When she'd said that she knew nothing about Mum's diary, was she being entirely honest?

I saw them only once over the next three weeks, when I bumped into them outside the house. Elsa was already sitting in the car. Bettina looked concerned.

'I'm taking her to the doctor's again. Her cough sounds awful, and she's complaining about not being able to breathe properly.'

'Really sorry to hear that. Anything I can do to help?'

'Thank you. Maybe next week? I've taken this week off to look after her. I'll let you know.'

'Oh … just in case you're interested and can spare an hour or so, we're having a panel discussion on eyewitness accounts in the History department on Friday – considering how valuable and reliable they are. There's a buffet lunch afterwards. I'd be very pleased if you came along.'

'Can I let you know later? I've got to go now.'

The lecture theatre was filling up slowly, leaving quite a few vacant seats. However … not a bad turnout for the last day of term. Many of my students were in the audience, plus colleagues from other departments, but not a sign of Bettina. Sam and I took our seats on the raised podium. He reminded the audience of the usual format of the discussion – a ten-minute introduction, followed by questions and answers, a buffet lunch. Then it was my turn to give the introduction.

'In a recent Reith Lecture, Hilary Mantel said, "If we

want to meet the dead, looking alive, we turn to art." A little later, she states, "As soon as we die, we enter into fiction. Just ask two different family members about someone recently gone ... Once we can no longer speak for ourselves, we are interpreted. And when we remember, we don't reproduce the past, we create it." *We* believe that the general sense of this statement holds true for historical events, but also for eyewitnesses of past events who are still alive. As historians, we are fully aware that we need to treat such accounts with a certain amount of scepticism, for these statements are all too often made with an eye to how future generations will judge them. Therefore, they are polished, cleansed and sometimes apologetic in tone. Although true records in the eye of the beholder, they are nevertheless recreated from memory, so need to be carefully interpreted.'

I briefly resumed eye contact with the audience, took a swig of water, then cleared my throat.

'In our book *Fractured Lives* we focus on the end of the Second World War, and take a from-the-bottom-up approach, using narratives from German eyewitnesses. We wanted to write the history of ordinary people – to historicise them, put them into the social structures and long-term trends that shaped their lives, but at the same time resurrect what they said and did. The historian Lord Macaulay once said: "History has to be burnt into the imagination before it can be received by the reason." So, let's discuss whether *you* think the history of ordinary people adds any value to traditional historiography. Who would like to kick off?'

I scanned the audience for raised arms. 'Professor

McCloud.'

'Thank you for your captivating introduction. I agree with you that such narratives are both problematic and promising. But do you not you think that this approach to history – the history of everyday life – may be seen by your critics as an attempt to normalise the Third Reich?'

'Dr Beckhard? Would you like to take this question?' Sam moved the microphone over to his side.

'This may partially hold true for stories recounted by second and third post-war generations, but I think to a much lesser degree if you listen to actual eyewitness accounts. However, you're right in saying that they're not without their problems. All narratives have a personal spin – most of them try to justify the narrator's actions or make them appear in a positive light. Nonetheless, personal accounts have redeeming merits because they record an individual's journey. The focus on a particular life offers more concrete detail than structural generalisations. Moreover, those unrecorded stories die alongside their authors. As Dr Berger said in his introduction, you always have to read between the lines, look for what is left out and fill in the gaps. And, last but not least, listening to eyewitnesses greatly expands one's own perspective on the war. It illuminates the human dimension, revealing an extraordinary mix of initial enthusiasm during the early victories in the war, followed by disillusionment and prolonged suffering.'

'Thank you. A question now from the student audience. Yes, Marcus.'

'Thanks. A question for Dr Berger. You said in your introduction – or, rather, quoted from Hilary Mantel –

that if we want to meet the dead, looking alive, we turn to art. Would you define history as an art or a science?'

'A very good question, which deserves a much more detailed answer than I can give here. But, in a nutshell, I will say this. Historic research uses various academic disciplines and merges them to get to know and understand historical events better – for example, the methods and some of the skills we use come from the social sciences, such as statistics, sampling and interviewing techniques. The art of our academic discipline is the ability to interpret and reassemble primary and secondary sources in order to offer more insight into and understanding of historical events. If you're seeking the safety and authority of pure science, history is the wrong place to look. History is in a constant state of flux, of self-questioning. So some scholars think of history as an art, whereas others consider it to be a social science, or both. H. Stuart Hughes' *History as Art and as Science* discusses this in detail. It's on your reading list.'

A few more questions followed regarding our methodological approach, eyewitness selection and whether our 1920s sample was a representative one.

All of a sudden, someone in the back row stood up and spoke.

'May I ask one more question, please?' Bettina must have slipped in late, unnoticed by me, and was now keen to ask a question.

'Yes, we'll take one last question before we break for lunch. The lady at the back ...'

'Does the panel believe that a historian with your particular skill set would be more or less biased when it comes to researching his own family history?'

I stepped down from the podium. As I contemplated my response, I paced a few steps to one side and back again, like a caged animal.

'Let me answer your rather personal question in an equally personal way. My chief concern is to understand what, and why, my parents did what they did within the social and political framework of their youth. I know from history what the great *majority* of the people did, but I can't know what they thought, as individuals, and how those thoughts influenced their actions. Therefore, I interpret on the basis of what I know about my parents and fill in the gaps with likely assumptions, just as one would in the first phase of developing a film in a darkroom. There is no light and you have to feel the end of the film roll, take a snip in the dark and hope for the best. Then you slowly begin to develop the pictures, analyse them and draw your conclusions. In the end, you can't separate fact from fiction. It's the story that evolves, the story as you see it – maybe even as you want to see it. Call it a cathartic absolution, or a posthumous cutting of the mental umbilical cord.'

There was brief, but audible, applause.

Sam concluded the meeting. 'I'd like to thank you all for coming. Lunch is now being served next door, in room one ten.'

'So, that's Bettina,' Sam said. 'What was she getting at with her question? I thought you handled it pretty well.'

'I'm not sure. I find she blows hot and cold. I can't make her out, really. Ooh, here she comes. Hi, Bettina. So glad you could come. May I introduce Sam, my friend and coauthor.'

'Good to meet you, Bettina. I hope you can stay for lunch.'

'Just for a few minutes. I need to get back to my aunt. She's really not well at the moment.'

An English department colleague, plus a few of my students, came up to the podium, bombarding me with more questions. Sam and Bettina went ahead to have lunch.

An hour later, Sam came up to me, grinning. Bettina had already left.

'Guess what? She's coming to the end-of-term party tomorrow!'

'You're such a flirt.'

'No, I'm just ploughing the field a bit. You'll have to do the sowing.'

'God, that's so sexist!'

'It's called "corriger la fortune". Anyway, I'm glad term's ended. I'm off. See you tomorrow.'

That evening, I went back to my house to check my post and answerphone. Helmut's partner had left a message for me two days earlier. 'Hi, it's Gisela. We have some worrying news, I'm afraid. Helmut's in hospital with kidney failure. He's on dialysis and the doctor said that it can only be stopped when his kidneys recover. At this point, we don't know if it's a temporary problem or whether he'll need a transplant. Apparently, there's a long donor waiting list. Don't worry too much. We'll keep you posted, of course. Bye for now.'

My heart was racing as I deleted the message. As far

as I knew, Helmut had none of the early symptoms, like swollen hands or feet, but maybe he'd just not wanted to worry me. I Googled 'kidney donor' instantly. My palm felt clammy as I moved the mouse around the screen. *Donor compatibility is established through blood tests that look for matching blood types and antigens*, I read. Apparently, siblings have a one in four chance of being an exact match.

Chapter 15

Bettina once asked me whether I was an introvert or an extrovert. I told her that I saw myself as an introverted extrovert – I love meeting new people, talking to them, sharing different experiences, but I also need my alone time. About six months ago, on an 'away day', the university encouraged us to fill in a personality type questionnaire as a way of fostering teamwork among colleagues – 'creating synergy' was the buzz phrase at the time. I was deemed to be an INTJ personality type, meaning that on the Extrovert–Introvert scale I tended towards the latter. I also favoured Thinking over Feeling and Judging over Perceiving. There was another category, too, but I don't remember what it was. The report summed me up as being interested in ideas and theories. Apparently, INTJs always question why things happen the way they do. They are excellent at developing plans and strategies, and don't like uncertainty.

I've always taken this kind of test with a large pinch of salt. It's a bit like reading your horoscope. Of course I don't like uncertainty! Nobody does. I didn't like not knowing whether Helmut would make a full recovery or – if worst came to worst – if I'd be a suitable donor. I also wasn't clear about the risks and consequences for both of us in case he needed an operation.

When I rang the hospital, Helmut was still on dialysis. We'd have more conclusive results over the next forty-eight hours, they said.

Where was the relationship with Bettina heading? It had moved from cool standoffishness to a budding friendship – or maybe more. Since we'd been out together at the concert, I'd noticed that she had started to make more of her appearance – eye shadow, mascara, blusher. Each time I saw her, she was wearing a different outfit and had her hair done in a slightly different way. Unexpectedly, I found myself looking forward to seeing her again, although I still had some misgivings. I'd entered their house under false pretences, and although we'd agreed to play 'no more charades' I hadn't been entirely open about my reasons for launching myself into their lives.

And then there was 'the other issue'. She was much younger than me, and a man past fifty ought to know better than continue to attach importance to love affairs. I had no time and no energy for emotions or responsibilities. Work had always come first, and for a while I stubbornly continued in the role I had long assigned myself – the detached friend, rather than boyfriend or lover.

Saturday beckoned. Party time. Bettina and I shared a taxi to Sam's. A cool shower was pelting down on the taxi's roof and bonnet, steaming up the windows. While the driver demisted the windscreen with a burst of warm air, we made no effort at all to clear our windows. We just leaned back in the mild, misty cocoon, shielded from the outside world.

'Wow! Two Saturday nights out in a row – what have I done to deserve this?' There was a shade of coquetry in her voice. And this time it was *her* hand that gently brushed and closed over mine. I couldn't decide whether this was an amorous gesture or one born out of gratitude.

'It's all Sam's fault. And yours, of course, for turning up to the panel discussion,' I said, trying to suppress a faint smile of complicity.

A deafening bass boom echoed through Sam's quiet residential street in Muswell Hill. The party was already in full swing.

We linked arms as we went in.

'Ah, the good-looking couple!' Sam ushered us into the hallway. 'Come on in – straight ahead to the kitchen. That's where all the drinks are. And most of the guests.'

I cast a passing glance into the living room. A few people stood around chatting in small clusters in the unusually tidy room. No books or newspapers, no longer toys strewn across the floor. Ruth and Sam had carted the children off to their grandparents, so they wouldn't be disturbed by boisterous partygoers. In the kitchen, the noise level was more bearable and none of the guests were smoking there. I could hear colleagues from the History department chatting away as we approached.

' … awkward question at the end. Who was that woman?'

'Don't know. But his reply was very candid. *Here* he is. Hi, Jonas. You OK?'

'Hi, Barbara. Colin! Good to see you. I hope you enjoyed the panel discussion. This is Bettina – she works at the British Library.'

Raucous laughter cut the introductions short. Heads turned. Not far away, near the buffet, stood the Dean, who was entertaining colleagues with some of his jokes. He was well known for exploding into foolish hilarity, way before he reached the punchline. He mumbled on intermittently to the last part of the joke, whilst stuffing his face with canapés and washing them down with Claret. The polite response from his audience sounded like canned laughter. I wanted to move as far away as possible, fearing I'd be questioned about our progress on *Fractured Lives*. He'd ask me whether we had a definite publication date to put in the Research Assessment Exercise. That's all he was interested in.

'Excuse me, I'll just say hello to our hostess …'

'Sam told me about your new friend,' Ruth said. 'She sounds very nice. Is it serious?'

'We're just friends.'

'I thought you'd already moved in with her?'

'Well, not exactly. I live in the same house, it's just—'

'Sorry, I didn't mean to pry. You'd better go and rescue her from Sam's clutches – they're dancing in the conservatory.' The uncirculated air on the crowded dance floor smelled of sweat and deodorant. Bettina spotted me as I opened the patio door to let in some air.

'Jonas, come on. Salsa music – one of my favourites. It's "Valió la Peña". Come and dance.'

Gyrating her hips to the fast rhythm of the music, her arms stretched out, she tried to lure me on to the dance floor. This was a side of Bettina I hadn't seen before. To be able to move like that, she must have had dance lessons.

Sam was out of breath and somewhat relieved when I took over – reluctantly. I tried to copy her steps but was conscious of my awkward dance moves. Fortunately, the next piece was a cha-cha-cha, one of the few dances I remembered from my youth.

'Not bad,' she said, when we added the New York basic steps. 'And apparently you're not just an academic.' There was that coquettish tone again.

'How so?'

'Sam told me you've been writing poetry.'

'He's such a bigmouth. I wouldn't believe everything he says.'

'Have you, or haven't you?'

'Maybe.'

'In which case, you have. Will you let me read some?'

A slow dance followed. We swayed gently to the tune of the music – my hands around her hips, hers clasped around my neck – our bodies just brushing, tactile, but not too close. I loved her delicate sandalwood perfume.

Closing my eyes, I remembered my first slow dance as a fifteen-year-old, dancing in close embrace with a pretty seventeen-year-old I had never met before. She'd deliberately rubbed her pelvis against my crotch, causing me excitement and embarrassment in equal measure.

'Will you?' Bettina whispered her repeated question, tilting her cheek against mine. I hesitated, as if to consider her request for the first time.

'Will I what?'

'Let me read some of your poems?'

I stopped moving to consider her plea, then stumbled and nearly trod on her feet.

'Maybe.'

She took her arms from around my neck, placed her hands against my shoulders and pushed me back a few inches. I grasped both her hands, put them back round my neck, then pulled her closer.

'May I kiss you?' The sentence came out of nowhere. We held each other's gaze until her eyes answered my question. We kissed briefly. Then kissed again – long and passionately. We left the dance floor, helped ourselves to more drinks from the kitchen and, for a while, reluctantly mingled with the other guests.

The rain had stopped, which meant the air had cleared as we stepped out into the garden, arm in arm, to inhale the fresh breeze.

'Not quite spring yet,' Bettina said, breathing the air in deeply. Her teeth were chattering. I took off my jacket and wrapped it round her shoulders.

'I have no idea where this is going,' she said, leaning her head against my shoulder.

'Does it have to go anywhere?'

'Perhaps.'

I sensed she was a little disconcerted by my reply. 'I think we'd better make a move soon. I don't want to leave my aunt for too long. She's not well.'

An hour later, we said our goodbyes, following other guests on their way out. Sam stood at the door, hands in pockets, smirking.

'Hope you two had a good time. Thanks for coming.' Then, suddenly he conjured up a bottle of Champagne out of nowhere. 'The bet, remember?' And, just mouthing, he added, 'For later.'

'Lovely party. Thank you,' Bettina said, as we left. And, turning to Sam, she added, 'Valió la peña!'

'Shhh, you'll wake Auntie.' Bettina stopped me singing bits of the tune I'd picked up from 'Valió la Peña'. She closed the front door quietly behind me.

'Good,' she whispered. 'This time, you remembered that you live here! I'll just go and check she is alright. Would you mind making us some coffee?'

She pulled off her heels and tiptoed along the corridor. I put the kettle on and sat down in the kitchen. Then, all of a sudden, I heard the shower turning on upstairs. I imagined Bettina shedding her clothes, item by item, discarding skirt, blouse and knickers in a small pile, bra on top, until she was naked. I listened to the water pelting against the shower door. For a few minutes I contemplated joining in, but banished the thought. She wasn't that kind of woman – or was she?

I was rather taken aback when Bettina returned wearing nothing but a fluffy white bathrobe.

'Elsa's fast asleep. Sorry, but I had to have a quick shower. I was still sweating when we got back – I'm just not used to dancing all evening. Thanks for the coffee.'

I was wondering what was going through her mind. She hadn't exactly crafted the perfect pick-up line by asking *me* to make the coffee. And she'd ignored the bottle of Champagne I had placed in full view on the kitchen table. She just sat there sipping her coffee, legs crossed but revealing quite a bit of bare skin – a sight that can burn a potent image into a receptive man's mind. She looked sensual and seductive in her short bathrobe.

'When you said "valió la peña" to Sam, what did you mean? Do you speak Spanish?'

'A little. It means "it was worth it".'

She rose from her chair and came over to sit on my lap, tilting her head for a kiss.

'You were very sweet at the party, but asking for permission to kiss me was a bit old-fashioned.'

We kissed again and her mouth responded with increasing desire. I didn't ask for permission as my searching hands slipped inside the top of her bathrobe. Currents of desire and excitement that I had not known for years flooded over me. She pulled away, adjusting her robe and, putting a finger to her lips, led me upstairs to her room.

A few minutes later, we were lying on her bed, naked, arms and legs entwined. Neither of us spoke. Soft lips and caressing hands were gently lapping our bodies like shallow sea water. Then Bettina eased herself slowly out of the embrace and began to kiss my chest and body. She pushed me gently backwards onto the pillow, climbed on top and arched herself rhythmically as though her hips were moving independently of the rest of her body. Her eyes had closed – she began to tremble and breathe heavily, tossing her head from side to side.

'Oh my God, please. Yes, please! Yes, I'm …' Her breathing was so ragged that it was hard to make out the words. Gradually, her forward-tilting movements slowed down. Then there was a long silence. As she arched her body forwards onto mine, her pulse was no longer racing but steady and calm. I lifted her off, gently rolling her on to her front.

'And now—'

'You may,' she cut off my sentence with a teasing smile.

She had this wanton, playful way of reacting, just vaguely

hinting at things, leaving the rest to the imagination, offering pleasure beyond my wildest dreams. She trusted and desired me. We drifted into uncharted seas, the swell of passion carrying us to a place where we lost contact with the world. It was as if life was suspended, hovering on the cusp between one sensual state and another. When I rolled off her, we both lay face down across the bed. Bettina had pulled up the sheet, coyly covering us like post-coital film stars. She moved her face closer so that her lips and tongue could meet with mine, and then the sweet-tasting kisses gently faded away.

I can't remember how long we slept. Birdsong filtered in from outside. The sensation of warm blood returned to my heavy limbs, when I heard Bettina's feeble voice, seemingly from far away.

'I'm famished.'

Neither of us stirred. We remained in the same position, spooned together, peaceful and complete.

'Me too,' I croaked, after another lapse. My throat felt dry and sore.

'I think I'm falling in love,' she whispered into the pillow, as if the words were too fragile to be uttered aloud, 'but I'm still dying of hunger.'

'So am I,' I said, having regained my voice.

'Which one – in love or hungry?'

'A bit of both, I think. We should get up and have some breakfast,' I said, not moving.

'You first,' she breathed. 'I can't move just yet.'

We lay for a long time, amazed and unsure, without speaking. Her utterance from earlier on flashed across my mind – 'I have no idea where this is going.'

Outside, heavy rain mixed with hail beat against the shutters. In the distance, on the main road, tyres hissed on the waterlogged asphalt.

Bettina spent most of Sunday morning looking after her aunt, fixing her breakfast and administering the drugs the GP had prescribed for her. I went downstairs to say hello. Elsa was fiddling with her pipe, tamping down the tobacco with her index finger and testing its draw by sucking on it noisily. Drawing in the air triggered a long coughing fit. Bettina ran her hands through her hair in despair.

'Will you *please* put that pipe away. You heard what the doctor said.'

No comment. Instead, Elsa pushed the packet of drugs disdainfully to one side. 'These tablets make me all drowsy. I can't concentrate, and we need to finish the writing.'

'I can do a bit more typing this afternoon, when you've had a nap. In the meantime, no more smoking, and certainly no more Schnapps. Understood?'

'Can I help with anything? I asked Bettina. 'You could borrow my laptop.'

'No, this is private,' Elsa butted in. 'You can read it when I'm dead.'

Charming! I looked at Bettina, who just shrugged her shoulders.

'Fancy going out for lunch?' I asked.

Elsa gave her a disapproving look.

'Yes, I'd like that. See you a bit later. I'll sort out her lunch first.'

The menu at Antonio's listed most standard dishes you'd

expect in an Italian restaurant. However, almost every dish was described using mouth-watering adjectives like 'rich', 'thick', 'gooey', 'succulent', 'creamy' or 'frothy', in a way that reflected the owner's exuberant character. The simple minestrone soup was *butter-laced with a Cognac-kissed suavity*, a plate of gamberetti was *sautéed with chilli flakes and served with a salad of oyster mushrooms*, and the fresh fruit salad came *decorated with an airy crunch of meringue at the edges*.

We didn't really need any spicy zing to remind us of our first night together; it was still uppermost in our minds. Even watching Bettina eat her lunch created a certain 'pleasures at the table' atmosphere. I know that staring at someone while they eat is considered rude. But there was a definite sensual appeal in watching her slide her spoon slowly into the soft panna cotta, or scooping the froth off her cappuccino and seductively licking the spoon. It almost seemed like a purposeful prelude. Bettina gave me an innocent look.

'What?'

'Nothing – I just like watching you.'

'It's rude to stare.'

'Sorry.' I straightened up in my chair. 'Can I ask you something? You were quite firm with your aunt this morning, but still prepared to help her. Do you enjoy typing up her memoirs, or do you do it more out of a sense of duty?'

She put her dessertspoon down, dabbed the corners of her mouth with her serviette and pushed the unfinished panna cotta to one side.

'She's not exactly a reformed character, as I may have

told you before,' she said, avoiding eye contact. 'So, no, it's not really enjoyable at all. Fortunately, her memoirs are almost finished. She writes about the last year of the war mainly, but then there are these flashbacks to the "good old BdM days": playing scavenger hunt in the forest, singing by the campfire, enjoying the handicrafts workshop, and so on. It all seems so harmless.'

'Sounds familiar. My mother wrote glowingly about the BdM in *her* memoirs, but at least the second half of hers showed some critical reflection.'

'There's none of that. Elsa always says she wants to put things right. I don't know what she means by that. Sometimes she locks herself in her study for hours on end. I suspect she reads old letters and diaries. Pure nostalgia.'

Bettina sipped at her cappuccino and wiped a trace of froth from her lips. I moved my hand over hers on the table, caressing it gently. She put down her napkin and smiled.

'I wish I could just spend half a day in her study and explore some of those important sources. There may even be letters from my mother. It would be fascinating to compare your aunt's memoirs with hers.'

'I don't know, Jonas. If she finds out—'

'She won't. I can keep a secret. I promise. It'll be *our* secret. Just like she doesn't know about us.'

She withdrew her hand and reached for her purse. At least this time she hadn't said, 'The study door is always locked.' Did Bettina have a spare key? Did she know what else was in there?

When I offered to pay, she said, 'Let's go Dutch. You see, if you are a single woman like me, going to lunch or dinner with a man and you don't pay your share, it feels like he'll expect something in return. At least, that's how I feel – and I think it's better to manage your expectations.'

'And what expectations would those be?' I asked cheekily, knowing full well that she had other plans for the afternoon.

On the way home – we walked hand in hand for the first time – I explained to her about Helmut's kidney failure and how I needed to go abroad for a few days to see him.

'I'm so sorry. Have you only just heard? Gosh, I hope he'll be alright. Do you think he'll need a transplant?'

'We don't know yet, but I have to get some tests done – to see if I'm a suitable donor.'

'That's so brave of you. Can people live a normal life with just one kidney?'

'I should imagine so, but I haven't really done any research. But what does it matter, if it saves his life … ?'

She turned round to hug and kiss me. When I responded a bit too passionately, she said, 'Perhaps tonight – not now.'

Later that afternoon, I heard the by-now-familiar clatter of the typewriter. It continued for almost two hours. When it fell silent, I waited in vain for steps approaching my room. It wasn't until after midnight that I finally heard a faint knock on my door.

'Are you still up?'

'Yes, come in.'

'I'm sorry, but Elsa's condition seems to be getting worse. She says she can't breathe, and has these awful coughing fits. I had to sit beside her bed till she fell asleep. I'm really worried about her.'

I took Bettina in my arms and started to massage her temples. After a while, she pulled away and sat on my bed.

'I'm exhausted. May I stay with you tonight?'

'Of course. I'd like that.'

Later on, she whispered into the pillow: 'You will let me know how you get on with your brother, won't you? Any news, good or bad. And please come back soon.'

Chapter 16

The rush-hour traffic was horrendous. We were sitting bumper to bumper in the heavy rain, occasionally crawling forwards a few yards, then limping hopelessly from one red traffic light to another. Gisela, Helmut's partner, had kindly offered to drive us to the hospital. She'd booked his haemodialysis treatment and, at my request, had made an appointment for a kidney donor test. Helmut's initial dialysis results had been inconclusive. Thus, the doctors suggested continuing his treatment for another week – three sessions, each lasting three hours.

I was in the back of the car, studying the information that I had downloaded from the internet: *Living Donation – What You Need to Know*. I was about to start the section on *Surgery and Recovery* when we came to a complete standstill. It was gridlock, and soon every engine was turned off, drivers wound down their windows and stuck their heads out for clues. Then came the sirens – both police and ambulance – vehicles trying in vain to shoot through the dense traffic. Some drivers were listening to the radio, barely noticing the screaming sirens from behind that forced oncoming traffic to veer onto the kerb. We settled back in our seats. It was going be a long wait.

The day had hardly begun and Helmut already felt drowsy and tired. He was in a cantankerous mood. 'We're going to be late. Why did you have to go through town? You should have gone via the ring road.'

'There's been an accident,' Gisela said calmly. 'Nothing

we can do about it now. It's normally quicker through town.'

'Yeah, but not in rush hour on a Friday.'

'Oh, shut up, Helmut. You can do the driving next time – if you're up for it, that is. You always know better.'

'Why are we dragging Jonas out, as well? We should wait for the results first. I might not need a transplant at all. I just don't know why we're doing this *now*.'

'There's always a shortage of donors,' I chipped in. 'You could be waiting a long while. It's good to find out whether I'd be a suitable donor – just in case.'

'Yes, and stop being a grumpy old man. You should be grateful that you've got such a nice brother.'

When the stop–start driving resumed, Gisela reached forwards to turn the air-flow to internal circulation only. The traffic continued to move slowly down the winding road to the hospital like a long, angry snake, tyres hissing on the waterlogged asphalt.

A short while later, I was filling out a health questionnaire, clipboard on lap. When asked about medical conditions that would prevent me from becoming a donor, such as uncontrolled high blood pressure, diabetes, cancer, HIV, hepatitis and acute infections, I ticked all the *No* boxes. What followed – and which took most of the day – was an unexpectedly long process of assessment: complete medical history, physical examination, X-ray, ECG, urine test, and finally the all-important blood test to check for compatibility. If our blood types were compatible, further blood tests would be required for tissue typing and crossmatching. Great! Perhaps I should have listened to Helmut, after all, and waited for his dialysis results.

On the way home, I asked him why he hadn't told anybody about his illness before. He must have had some symptoms. 'Why didn't you say anything the last time I saw you?'

Silence.

'I wouldn't worry about it, Jonas. He doesn't tell me, either. I only discovered the other day that he'd made his will and paid for his own funeral costs.'

Helmut had his eyes closed and pretended not to be listening. I tapped him on the shoulder. 'You are a bit of a dark horse, Helmut. What else haven't you told us? Already got a spare kidney in the freezer, have we?'

Even when we were children, he'd always had his little secrets. He knew that Dad wasn't on the frontline in the war. In his teens, he'd stashed away Dad's 1945 registration card from the Military Government, and only a few months ago he'd handed me Dad's shocking letter about his appalling near-death experience. To top it all, I discovered after Mum's funeral that he'd been giving Elsa legal advice without telling me. He also knew where she lived.

When we got home in the evening, while Gisela was out getting us a take-away, Helmut indicated that he felt humbled by my offer to be his kidney donor, although he didn't say so in as many words.

'I appreciate what you're doing for me, Jonas. I hope it won't be necessary.'

'You know, reading all this stuff about the transplant procedure, I still have no idea what a kidney actually looks like. How big is it? Do you know?'

'I think it's the size of a small fist, shaped a bit like a hand grenade. You should know all about that,' he laughed.

'Yeah, I remember … Long time ago. Got big brother *really* scared when I found it in the rubble.'

'Well, you nearly blew us all up; it was still live.'

Gisela returned with three generous portions of souvlaki and chips. 'What are you two talking about – boys' stuff, is it? Beer, Jonas?'

'Please,' Helmut answered.

'Yes, dear. You'll have cranberry juice – special treat for your kidneys.'

He frowned and began recounting the hand grenade story in greater detail – how I'd hidden it under the bed, then threatened to pull the trigger before he coaxed me into handing it over. There was this rather heroic older brother spin on his story which I disliked.

Gisela got up to answer the house phone in the hall.

'Helmut – it's for you,' she shouted.

'Who is it?'

'I don't know. She wouldn't give me her name.'

When Helmut returned, his food had gone cold. 'It was Mum's old friend Elsa. She asked me whether I'd had a successful operation. How the hell does she know about it?'

'Oh, Bettina must have told her. I mentioned you'd been in hospital.'

'Who the fuck is Bettina?'

Helmut impaled two cold soggy chips on his fork, chewed them, then pushed the whole plate away in disgust.

'She's Elsa's niece. You know – Tina. They live together.

We are—'

'An item? I don't believe this. Are you sleeping with her to get to Elsa?'

'What's all this about?' Gisela interjected.

'Jonas has got this fixation with Mum's old war diary, which might not even exist any longer, and may prove nothing at all. He's also sniffing around in their house to find evidence of Elsa having worked in a POW camp during the war – allegedly.'

'*Concentration* camp. She worked in one as a guard. Was part of the killing machine … Yes, and I'm getting very close to uncovering the truth, as a matter of fact.'

'Elsa's aware of the change in the law. She's anxious that—'

'What change?' Gisela jumped in.

'You no longer have to prove that an intentional act directly leads to a killing. According to the new law, actively working in a death camp is punishable. She's really frightened, Jonas. She thinks they might extradite her if they find out where she lives. For God's sake, is that what you're planning?'

'No. At least, not yet. And it's not for me to judge whether there's sufficient evidence that she was working there at the time. I just want to establish the facts.'

'I wish you'd stop digging up the past all the time. She's a frail old woman.'

'And *I* wish you'd stop helping her by finding legal loopholes.'

'You really do want her to be extradited, don't you? What would that achieve?'

'It would mean that justice is served. Justice for the

victims of the Holocaust. Justice for the survivors and their families.'

For a split second I visualised Helmut and two other judges in their black robes, sitting at the front of the courtroom, a juror on either side of them. The defendant Elsa and her lawyer sat on a bench to their right. And, in front of them, in the witness box, an elderly Jewish survivor.

Helmut pursued his argument about 'the intention to kill', referring to the twenty-year statutory limitation for manslaughter. Did people in Elsa's situation have any choice but to work in a camp, he wondered. According to him, they were just obeying orders for fear of imprisonment or even execution. I pointed out that obeying orders under duress was a post-war invention, a convenient line of defence and hopeful exoneration. Historians like Christopher Browning and Mary Fulbrook had convincingly demonstrated that, as a rule, refusal to participate in mass killings did not result in serious adverse personal consequences. We simply couldn't agree and Gisela refused to play the neutral arbiter.

I left two days later. Neither the results from the dialysis nor those from the donor test had come through. Helmut promised to ring me with any news.

Coming home to London late Friday night – my flight had been considerably delayed – I expected the house to be dark and quiet. Instead, I heard Bettina and Elsa screaming at each other in high-pitched voices.

Elsa was sitting in her usual armchair, clinging on to a

half-empty bottle of Schnapps; Bettina was leaning over her trying to wrench it out of her hands.

'Will you let go – *please*! And stop gibbering. I can't understand what you're saying.'

Elsa jabbered on incoherently. She was deliriously drunk. '… They're coming for me … The letter, see … I saved as many as possible, sending them to the factories … Don't let them in.' Then she stared at me and shouted. 'Impostor! Get him out. Helmut's going to help me.'

Bettina finally dragged the bottle away from her aunt and asked me to help lift her out of the chair.

I tried to calm her down. 'We're going to walk you to your room, Elsa. There's nothing to be afraid of. We're *all* here to help you.'

But she reeked of alcohol and could barely stand up, let alone walk, so we carried her to her bedroom, one of her arms around each of our shoulders. The second we lay her down on the bed, she made an explosive snorting noise and fell asleep. Bettina pulled up her duvet and turned out the light.

'I really don't know what caused that outburst. She's been like it for the past two days, getting drunk in the evening. What am I supposed to do?'

I grabbed a tissue, drew her towards me and wiped away her tears, dabbing gently at her running mascara.

'I can't take it much longer, Jonas … I've taken next week off work.'

'I'm really sorry I couldn't be here to help. Shall I make us some coffee?'

'Don't worry. I need something stronger, I reckon. I'll get myself a large gin and tonic. Sorry to burden you with this … How's your brother?'

Following her into the living room, I explained that we still didn't know if he needed a transplant. Nor had the donor test results come back. I didn't mention that Elsa had been talking to Helmut on the phone. Would this be a good moment to come clean? Or would it scupper my chances to get access to Elsa's memoirs or to discover Mum's diary? When we settled down on the sofa, she rested her head on my shoulder, moving her hand over mine. There was that pleasant smell of sandalwood again. I kissed her on the cheek.

'Stay with me, stay with me tonight.' I felt her hand tightening around mine – it had a certain glassy fragility.

Bettina stirred first, and reached out a caressing hand. I propped myself up on my elbow and stroked her arm. Her skin was warm to the touch, like a soft peach in the sun. Timid beams of sunshine radiated through the half-open curtains. Our lips met briefly.

'You can come into the shower with me if you want.' I couldn't decide whether this was more than just a friendly gesture.

A little later, we were lying on the bed on our bath towels, bodies still wet, two lovers with their arms and legs entwined. Half the morning just slipped through the sheets.

Bettina glanced at her alarm clock. 'God, I have to check if Elsa's OK.' She jumped out of bed hastily.

'I doubt she'll be awake yet,' I said. 'She's probably still sleeping off the drink from last night. Come back to bed.'

Bettina returned half an hour later with a breakfast tray

– coffee, eggs, toast and almond croissants.

'Wow – magic! Breakfast in bed. I don't think I've ever had … Thank you so much.'

Bettina gestured for me to hold the tray, propped up the pillows, then slipped into bed beside me.

'Elsa didn't want to get up, or eat anything. She just asked for some headache tablets. She also wanted to know whether you'd gone – not sure why. I think she's going to stay in bed for the rest of the day.'

'Good. Shall we go out? How about a trip on Regent's Canal – go to Little Venice?'

'Ooh, I've never done that before. Good idea. Why not?'

The sun had broken through the fluffy white clouds by midday. Clumps of pansies in vibrant hues and swaying daffodils bathed in the warm spring breeze. There would be no rain today. A group of Chinese tourists in long coats, brollies at the ready, formed a queue at the quayside, waiting to embark.

Bettina looked lovely in her white cotton blouse, unbuttoned at the top, revealing quite a bit of cleavage. Her pink jacket was draped over her left arm, while her other held on to me. I hadn't bothered to take a jacket, wearing only a black polo neck and jeans. We bought tickets for the 2.15 trip before joining the queue.

'You buy ticket for ship before?' An elderly Chinese lady asked me.

'Yes, definitely. It's also much cheaper to buy them in advance – at the ticket office over there,' I lied.

The whole group followed her. Meanwhile, Bettina and I exchanged conspiratorial glances. We had now jumped to the front of the queue and would be able to choose our seats.

Lady Y was an ageing narrowboat, around forty-five feet long and seven feet wide, and garishly painted in green and yellow. Her paint was slightly flaking, though, and her original azure colour emerged a few inches above the waterline. Bettina and I sat in the open-sided foredeck, housing a long table and padded bench seats. There was only room for about six passengers. Luckily, the Chinese cohort decided to stay together and sit in the covered cabin area.

One of the crew untied the ropes and pushed the boat off the quay with his foot, legs momentarily straddling boat and riverbank. Just when we expected him to do the splits and end up in the water, he pulled his leg over at the very last moment. The boat lay steady in the water, slowly moving upstream past rows of elegant Regency-style houses.

'*Lady Y* welcomes you aboard. My name is Jimmy. I'm your skipper and tour guide. We're now leaving London's Little Venice, a very quiet canal area, and home to smart waterside cafés and plenty of pubs. I'll point out places of interest to you as we go along. We'll stop briefly at London Zoo, before carrying on to our final destination at Camden Town.'

'Is that the kind of house you're buying?' Bettina said, pointing to one of the Regency villas.

'Yes, it is. But that one is probably just out of my price range – about ten million pounds, I reckon. Will you come and stay in my new house?'

'Are we going *out*? You and I?'

'I don't know – are we?'

'Sam thinks we are.'

'I thought we were staying *in* tonight!' She took a cushion from the bench and threw it at me. I pulled her towards me and kissed her on the lips. I could tell from her reaction that she felt embarrassed kissing in public.

Now and then came an announcement from the skipper, pointing out the Narrowboat pub, the Canal Museum and other tourist attractions along the way, but it all fell on deaf ears. We just talked, and had eyes only for each other.

In the evening we cooked a meal together for the first time: sea bass, sautéed potatoes with spinach and halloumi salad. To be honest, I was more like the sous chef, preparing the fish and stuffing it with herbs and lemon.

'I rarely cook for me and Elsa. We tend to get ready meals or take-aways. She probably won't even like this, but I'd best ask her. Can you just switch everything off when the timer goes, please? I won't be a minute.'

My phone pinged with an email from Helmut.

Good news! The doctors think that I won't need a transplant after all and, given time and the right medication, I should make a full recovery. Just for your info, I've attached a letter from the hospital with the donor test results. It doesn't matter now, but you wouldn't have been a suitable donor anyway.

What a relief!

I started to read the hospital's long explanatory letter: haematology results, their values and interpretations, Y-chromosome tests, lots of medical terminology I didn't understand. I scanned most of it, then closed the document.

'Elsa just wanted a sandwich and went back to bed,' Bettina said, re-entering the room. 'So, it's just dinner for two tonight.'

'I've got some good news. Helmut's just emailed – he's OK, and won't need a transplant, after all. I'm so pleased.'

'That's brilliant. Maybe we should open a nice bottle to celebrate.'

We sat down to a delicious dinner and opened the 'bet'-winning Moët that Sam had handed to me after his party. Fortunately, Bettina didn't ask me about the non-existent wager.

'Cheers! And thanks for a lovely day.'

'Cheers – to us!'

I don't know whether it was the Champagne, the enjoyable day out or just the relaxed atmosphere that led Bettina to reveal her true feelings towards her aunt.

'You know, that woman is so deluded. She lives in the past and wants to rewrite history. The stuff she wants me to write down … Sometimes I think she's worse than the National Front.'

She instantly put her hand over her mouth. Her sentence had surprised herself as much as me. It was pure impulse. The words had just slipped out. I sensed she had no idea how *much* she wanted to separate from her aunt – no longer play this charade of protecting her, no matter the cost to her own sanity. Bettina straightened up, threw her head back, ran both hands through her hair, and then looked at me. A very different smile appeared across her face – this one was mischievous and conspiratorial. We'd only just finished our meal when she stood up and walked over to my side of the table.

'Come.' All traces of caution had vanished from her voice. The word sounded confident, even encouraging. It was like an announcement that she would show me something, invite me somewhere hidden and mysterious. There was an air of intimacy and complicity. She took my hand, put one finger to her lips, and led me upstairs to her bedroom.

'Help me push this wardrobe. Come – from this side.'

When we'd managed to shove it slowly to one side, a connecting door to Elsa's study revealed itself.

'Wow!'

'Ssh …'

As she turned the key, I sensed she was still unsure whether she really *should* let me enter this holy of holies. Once the door was finally unlocked, Bettina pushed it softly, as though visiting someone's sickroom. Only a crack at first, then she opened it wider, pushing against a number of objects littering the floor on the other side. I felt as if we were going back in time almost sixty years. A cool, eloquent silence prevailed – a room passively stuffed with frozen time. Although I was utterly certain that she wasn't there, I half expected to find Elsa bent over her desk, dictating from her diary. I took a very deep breath and stepped in.

Chapter 17

Bettina leaned against the doorframe, lingering for a moment to let me through. Concentration lines had appeared on her forehead – like she'd suddenly been confronted with an unpredictable situation that may have severe consequences. Was she having second thoughts? She said nothing. For a few seconds, she closed her eyes and ran both hands through her hair. Once she had herself under control again, she turned on the light.

Elsa's study looked like the room of an aged actress. It was a complete mess. Had she been using it as a dressing room, as well? Clothes were draped over various items of furniture; odd-looking bundles, shabby and soiled, were scattered everywhere. Next to a bookcase in the corner stood a stack of cardboard boxes, battered and bulging, one with a red arrow pointing downwards, *OPEN HERE*. The whole room smelled musty and damp.

At one end, a desk along with typewriter and chair faced towards the window; at the other, a chaise longue had a small Persian rug half-tugged under it. I scanned the rest of the room.

Then I saw it.

On the nest of tables, in a small silver frame: the picture of Elsa with Dad, both in uniform, happily smiling into the camera. The very photograph I'd seen when peering through the window some time ago. I picked it up and showed it to Bettina.

'You know that's my dad? He was probably about

twenty then. He and Elsa were sweethearts before he met my mum.'

'Really? I had no idea.' Bettina stood still for a moment, frowned in puzzlement, seemingly trying to make important connections. Then she walked over to a bookcase and picked up another small frame. This photo showed Elsa, at about the same age – sixteen or seventeen – holding a tiny baby.

'Elsa once told me that she'd had her lover's child when she was very young, and that she'd had to give it up for adoption. Heartbreaking … Do you think it—?'

'It could well be. God … A few weeks ago, when you were out of the room, I showed Elsa a picture of Mum and Dad dated May 1944. She pointed to the bulge in Mum's dress and said laconically. "She was the lucky one." It makes even more sense now.'

My head was spinning, my eyes and mouth gaping open, frozen. I stared at the black-and-white photo of young Elsa and her baby. 'But that would mean—'

'Exactly. That you and Helmut have a half-brother … somewhere. As far as I know, the child – I believe it was a boy – has never contacted her.'

She put the photograph back on the bookshelf, sat down next to me on the chaise longue and took my hand in hers.

'Has that upset you?'

'I … I just find it difficult to understand that my dad could have—'

'What? Had a relationship with my aunt? They were both very young. First love. It was wartime, and at that point Elsa hadn't even started working in the camp.'

'So you know about that, too?'

She let go of my hand. 'Yes, and I'm not proud of it. She worked for her husband in the camp. He was in charge.'

'Is there any evidence of this?'

'He was convicted at the Nuremberg trials. You know that.'

'No, I mean evidence of *her* working there?'

'I guess she must have been on the civil service payroll. It was a lucrative job for an unskilled worker. Guards earned twice as much as factory workers.'

Blood money, I thought, but didn't say anything. I needed to tread carefully. I didn't want her to suspect anything; that Sam and I were working towards having her aunt extradited. I also wondered if Helmut knew about our half-brother. It would explain his support for Elsa and how reluctant he was for me to 'dig up the past'.

I walked over to the two chest-high bookcases. Next to Hitler's *Mein Kampf* sat works by the Holocaust denier David Irving – *The Destruction of Dresden* and *Hitler's War*. 'Do you think she's read all of these?'

'Probably. She spends a lot of time in here.' Bettina began exploring the room herself, as though for the first time. 'I wasn't ever allowed to touch anything in this room. Look – have you seen these?'

Strewn over the bare floorboards were disorderly piles of discoloured newspapers. She picked up a dusty copy of *Der Stürmer,* a Nazi propaganda tabloid, from 1934. The strapline read *Die Juden sind unser Unglück!* – 'The Jews are our downfall!'

'Terrible. I don't know why she kept them,' she added.

'May I have a look at her diary?' I opened the desk

drawer, assuming I'd find it in there.

She glanced at me, raised her eyebrows, then shook her head. 'Over there.'

She took a large lacquered wood box down from the top of the other bookcase, its cover finely embellished with marquetry, then sat down at the desk. She lifted the engraved clasp and took out a booklet covered in brown leather, frayed at the edges. I had spotted this, too, a few weeks before, but I'd been unable to read any of the writing from so far away.

She gasped in surprise when she opened the booklet. All the pages had been ripped out, except for a few sheets at the end. 'I don't believe this!' We looked at each other, both equally perplexed. 'When did I last do any typing for her?'

'Sunday afternoon, I think, after we got back from Antonio's. I went to Germany the next day to see Helmut.'

'That's right. She did ask me to finish typing the last couple of pages of her memoirs when you were away, but I refused, because she'd started drinking again.'

I was fairly certain that Elsa had twigged that Bettina and I were having a relationship, but now wondered whether she suspected me of having an ulterior motive. Previously, when I'd shown an interest in her memoirs, she'd rudely remarked, 'You can read it when I'm dead.' And the fact that she'd now called me an impostor was a clear sign she didn't trust me any longer.

'She must have stashed the pages away somewhere. Maybe they're in her bedroom. I can ask her when I type up the rest for her tomorrow. But I still don't know why—'

'Bloody hell! Look at this ...' I'd leaned over her

shoulder to take a closer look. 'That's mum's handwriting! I swear it is. These pages must be from her diary. Look, your aunt's made so many deletions and additions. Mum always maintained that Elsa couldn't string two sentences together.'

'Are you absolutely sure these pages are from your mum's diary?'

'One hundred per cent.'

'I had no idea, Jonas. I'm really sorry. I thought she was editing her own diary – not sure why she always called them her memoirs.'

We both read through the heavily edited pages. Not only had Elsa sanitised whole passages to make them comply with Nazi ideology, but she'd also obliterated all Mum's doubts and criticisms of the Führer. She'd even inserted new phrases to obscure and contradict the original text, thus making a complete mockery of the diary. Bettina shook her head in disbelief.

'Now I understand what Elsa meant by "I want to put things right." Utterly shameful. She really has been rewriting history. You know, she always held the diary close to her chest, never let me see her writing or annotations when she dictated her text.'

'What about the dates in Mum's diary? Did she falsify those, too?'

'Yes, the dates are also wrong for Elsa's bio. She lied to me about the year she'd had her child. I should have twigged. I'm so sorry.'

There they were, the last two pages of Mum's war diary, mutilated almost beyond recognition.

6th June, 1944

A letter from mother has just reached me. Cologne has been ~~completely~~ destroyed, but most of us survived. She will come with me to Liegnitz after our wedding, as she wants to be with me when the baby is born. A son for the Führer! She tells me that we need to ~~flee to the West~~ withstand the Russian onslaught. Although the Western Allies have landed in Normandy ~~and~~ she hoped that the ~~dreadful~~ war will soon ~~be over.~~ be won.

7th June

I hope to see you soon, my love. I too have managed to get two days' leave for our wedding! How will we get to Cologne? Will the Allies have occupied Cologne by then? ~~Do you~~ I believe in the Führer's Wunderwaffen?.

31ˢᵗ January 1945

~~I'm so afraid.~~ We managed to get all our children on the last trains to the West a week ago. We can now hear Russian tanks pounding Kattowitz. As we set off on our arduous journey, ~~abandoning the region of~~ from Warthegau, we saw anti-tank barriers set up at major road intersections to stop the enemy. SS men checked our papers, ready to arrest and execute any deserters. Some were detained, others shot in front of our eyes. ~~Desertion suddenly seemed quite natural to me.~~ We passed a dead soldier with a sign around his neck saying, 'Here I hang because I did not believe in the Führer.'

~~Why~~ Hold out against overwhelming odds?! ~~We want~~ Our men ~~to~~ will come home, ~~I pray to God they will.~~ The time for heroism has ~~long since~~ not gone. ~~East Prussia and Silesia is lost for ever, I fear.~~

I still *believed in you, mein Führer,* ~~but you have betrayed us all with your empty promises.~~ *I* continue to *worked tirelessly for you and the Fatherland,* ~~but now I see I've worked for the Devil. For the first time I feel that I can hate, hate you for all the destruction and deaths you've caused.~~
Long live the Reich!

Did Elsa really believe all this garbage? Or was it more an act of belated revenge against a friend-turned-enemy for stealing her lover? Why else would someone spend so much time and effort on this elaborate and disgracefully simplistic fake? And where had she hidden all of the torn-out pages? I was still keen to read the original diary, even though it was now pockmarked with Elsa's scribbles.

The whole quest for Mum's diary had begun with a single torn-out page stuck loosely in a scrapbook, along with mementos from my childhood. Why is there only one page of the diary? I had asked myself back then. I wondered if Elsa had ripped it out and given it back to Mum. 'The Führer wouldn't have liked that from someone like you, fleeing from the Russians, in a long trek of desperate refugees,' she might have said. Too sad and defeatist for Elsa's liking, I guess.

We looked everywhere for the torn-out pages, rummaged around in her desk drawer, checked behind rows of books and even opened some of the sealed cardboard boxes lying on the floor.

'You won't find it there,' a voice hissed furiously from behind our backs. We stopped dead in our tracks. She had appeared out of nowhere. Elsa stood barefoot in the open door, dressed only in her oversized nightgown like a ghost waving her stick in anger. Flushed with rage, her gaze first met Bettina's, whose jaw dropped in a silent scream of horror.

'Scum. You're scum, the both of you! Now working together, are we? With your spying boyfriend – like father like son. Keep looking, but you'll never find it. I burnt it, bit by bit.'

I felt sweat drench my skin; my heart was thumping against my chest. My fingers were curled into a fist, nails digging into my palm. I was furious now. I should have taken the boy's words seriously when he'd warned me before my first visit to the house: 'The old witch burns things at night.' Finally, I gathered enough courage to answer her back.

'Why on earth did you destroy my mother's diary? And why did you falsify it? It's a useless fake now.'

'None of your business. You had no right to it. Your mother gave it to me,' she said, snatching the last few pages from her desk.

'Afraid of the future *and* the past, are we?' I goaded her.

'Don't, Jonas,' Bettina intervened.

'He's a liar, Bettina. An impostor. He's living here under false pretences. He's been on to the authorities – wants me sent back to Germany. I have the letter.' She shook her fist at me in rage.

'What letter?' Bettina asked.

'From the German Foreign Office. The Wiesenthal Centre was asking them to confirm my real name. I want him out! He's got his own place – I checked with Helmut.' Coughing and gasping for air, she held on to the back of the chair for support.

'Is this true, Jonas?' Bettina's face was white as a sheet.

'No, I haven't written to the Foreign Office. Sam may have contacted the—'

'I don't believe you. And have you really got your own place?'

'I can explain …'

Elsa collapsed into Bettina's arms. We carried her over to the chaise longue, where she lay convulsing and twitching.

'Quick, call an ambulance. And then *go* … Get out and don't ever come back.'

I caught her gaze briefly. Those kind eyes which only a short time ago were filled with so much purpose and love now exuded utter hatred and bitterness.

When the ambulance arrived, Bettina grabbed her coat. They fitted an oxygen mask over Elsa's face, took her pulse and carried her out on a stretcher. We followed the paramedics downstairs.

'Can we please talk later?' I said, putting my hand timidly on her shoulder.

'Don't touch me. Just get out!'

I walked all the way back to my house in West Hampstead, deeply ashamed and dejected. The light drizzle soon turned into heavy showers, which poured down relentlessly. No umbrella. For a while I sheltered in front of a shop window, hoping the rain would stop. In my reflection, I could see my hair dripping with water, bald patches showing through in several places. It kept bucketing down. I no longer cared, and walked on, stepping through the puddles. Soon I was drenched from top to toe and with every step my shoes squelched a melancholic sigh. I watched the torrents of water heading for the drains. Just like my relationship with Bettina, I thought. All going down the fucking drain.

At home I decanted two inches of rain water from the sleeve of my jacket into the sink and hung up the rest of my clothes to dry. What now? I thought a little later, sitting in a hot bath in a cold home, breathing in deeply through the nose in an effort to steady my nerves. However, guilt sat heavy on my chest like an ugly scar. There was no redemption in sight. My whole plan had gone seriously wrong. Although Bettina had finally taken me into her confidence and offered to help, she'd done so out of love. Did she not know that confidences can be dangerous, entangling – like fly-paper? Falling in love had not been not part of the plan. You didn't think of that either, Sam, or did you?

I paced up and down in the living room, willing the phone to ring. Nothing. Maybe she'll call me from the hospital? Maybe later. I told myself to keep calm, poured myself a large whisky and gulped it down in one. I fidgeted – taking my glasses off, then putting them back on. Then, from upstairs I fetched my notebook and my favourite silver pen. But the pen remained poised above the blank page. I just couldn't put into words what I felt, what I had experienced in the past few days.

Had I actually achieved anything by the end of the journey into my family's history? What had I discovered about their fractured lives? Yes, I'd finally traced a few remnants of my mother's diary, but it didn't really prove very much, other than that, by the end of the war, she felt betrayed by Nazi ideology. To my horror, the really interesting stuff – the main part of her diary and eyewitness account – had been destroyed.

Only fragments remained, scraps from which we derive our historical accounts. What kind of human being was she? A deluded member of the Nazi Party, brainwashed at the age of ten, who became a leading member of the BdM. When her world collapsed, what values did she have left? Which ones did she retain and pass on to us? Later in her life, she did see through the indoctrination, shedding the Nazi skin and becoming a Social Democrat, just like her mother.

I had established through my primary sources that – directly or indirectly – Dad had been involved in war crimes. Through the amorous adventures of his youth, he'd established a connection with Elsa, who had turned out to be an unrepentant war criminal.

I would like to have found evidence that your intelligence rendered you immune to the Fascist ideology, and that you never raised your arm in the Fascist salute. But both of you made a pact with the Devil and turned a blind eye to those crimes. Crimes for which there will never be an appropriate name, as long as we live.

Writing about your parents is not cathartic. The word I use is 'closure', but there *is* no closure. They are with you until the day you die.

I couldn't sleep that night. I got up and listened to Bach's entire *St Matthew Passion* for the very first time – a heartrending piece of music about guilt and atonement which touches everyone, religious or not.

I left a message on Bettina's phone, asking if I could pick up my stuff from the house on Sunday afternoon. When I called the next day, there was no one at home. So I packed all my belongings and left the keys on the kitchen table.

Chapter 18

One evening in the middle of May – I hadn't heard anything from her for three weeks – Bettina rang me at home. I was busy deleting unwanted files and emails from my PC in an attempt to regain some storage space.

'It's Bettina. Sorry to bother you. Could I have your brother's phone number, please?' Her voice sounded urgent and breathless.

'Bettina, what's wrong? Is it your aunt?'

'Yes, I'm really worried about her. She discharged herself from hospital two days ago and hasn't been home since. I thought she might have got in touch with Helmut.'

'Shall I ring him for you?'

'If you don't mind.'

'I'll do it now and call you straight back.'

There was no trace of Elsa. She hadn't been in touch with Helmut. He imagined that she'd gone underground for fear of extradition … and lay the blame fairly and squarely at my door.

I relayed this to Bettina. 'I'm sorry, but she hasn't been in contact with him. Have you rung the police to report her missing?'

'No. I'm not sure she'd want me to. Under the circumstances.'

'Listen, can we talk, please?'

'There's nothing more to say. But you can have your raincoat back. You left it in the downstairs wardrobe.'

'Oh, OK. When shall I come and pick it up?'

'I don't want you to come to the house ever again. I'll take it to work on Wednesday. You can collect it from there.' She hung up.

My index finger hit the Delete button on my PC several more times in short succession, purging email after email without checking their contents. I hovered over the next one. It was from Helmut and had a PDF attached – *Donor Test Results*. Originally, I'd only taken a cursory glance at it and had given up reading the detail once Helmut let me know he didn't need a transplant after all. The report said I wouldn't have been a suitable donor anyway, but I'd never asked myself why not. Having read the details this time, I drew a sharp breath. According to the DNA and blood tests, we neither shared the same blood group nor did we have the same Y chromosome. I knew what that meant, but Googled it anyway to be absolutely certain. All male children inherit their Y chromosome from their father, and these children will in turn pass it on to their children. This inheritance pattern means that males coming from the same paternal line will always share the same Y chromosome. The conclusion hit me like an electric shock: Helmut and I couldn't have the same biological father!

Delete, delete. I didn't want to know. Confusion, anger, disbelief – I wasn't sure *what* I felt. I sat staring at the screen, stunned and motionless. My heart was beating against a chest that felt hollow. Helmut's phrases began whirling around in my head, as if to haunt me.

'You don't really look like my brother,' he used to tease me when we were teenagers. And, later on, the warning:

'Not always a good place to go, the past – poking around in old papers and photographs, as you do.'

My bottom lip trembled. Tears welled up in my eyes. I tried to suppress them, but they defied me, running down my cheeks, and even reaching my shirt. How could she? I remembered the BdM photograph of Mum's standard-bearer, the blonde girl with plaits carrying the flag with the swastika and the words *Glauben und Rein Sein* ('Faith and Purity'). The Nazi indoctrination obviously hadn't had a lasting effect on her.

Helmut had never been certain about Mum's affair with our family doctor, but liked to speculate about the identity of my biological father. Would he still be alive? What would *his* past reveal? He could turn out to be another Dr Mengele, the infamous 'Angel of Death'.

No more family research. Better the devil you know ...

I wondered if Helmut had read the full hospital report, and imagined that he had, being such a stickler for detail. It went with his profession. What would he think about having *two* half-brothers now? Maybe he didn't know about Dad's affair with Elsa after all.

As I write the word 'Dad', I feel empty, betrayed. Could this explain the lack of closeness between us?

I clenched my fists and screamed obscenities at my parents. 'Bastards, both of you. What else did you hide from me in your darkroom? Have you stashed away photographs of my real dad, Mum? Just a platonic relationship, was it? Was I the slight accident at the end? And you, Dad, would you have even known that I'm not yours? Did she get her own back on you for your affairs?'

I know: one should not speak ill of the dead, but then

my real dad might still be alive. I felt some slight relief, though, that I didn't have a half-brother from Dad and Elsa's relationship. What a bloody mess.

I got up and took down from the shelf the shoebox of old photos – the one I'd rescued from Mum's flat – and rummaged through the pictures in the vain hope of coming across a picture of our GP, my real father. How old would he have been when I was born? Stop! What a ludicrous idea. How can you find a person you've never seen? Also, I doubt that Mum would have dared to keep any photos of him, were she even to have had any.

I came across photos of Dad and me which I'd seen before, and stared coldly at one that suggested a rare moment of closeness. The one where I was sitting on his knee – I must have been about eight – and he was teaching me simple code-making. I ripped up the photo into lots of tiny pieces and threw it in the bin.

Helmut rang back half an hour later. My first thought was that Elsa had got in contact with him.

'Jonas. Sorry, I forgot to ask you. Are you coming over for my birthday? My musician friends will be joining us for a gig, so it should be fun. Bring your guitar. I promise there won't be any new revelations – no more secrets between us.'

'I'd love to. I could do with a bit of cheering up. Bettina and I have broken up, plus I have only just read the hospital report properly. Are you not shocked that we're only half-brothers? How sad is that?'

'I always suspected it, so it didn't come as a massive surprise. It doesn't make any difference to me, to be honest.

You're still my annoying little brother who insists on digging up the past.'

'I had to, because you kept all your little secrets from me. For fuck's sake, we're supposed to be brothers ... Well, half-brothers. Why couldn't you be honest with me? I bet you knew about Dad's love child with Elsa, too.'

'Yes. And I felt sorry for her that she had to give him up for adoption. But I have no desire to find out about him. You're the only brother who matters to me. I'm sorry. I have no more secrets. Everything is finally out in the open.'

He paused for a moment. I heard him blow his nose loudly. Was he trying to disguise his breaking voice?

'Like you, Jonas,' he continued, 'I found it difficult to love Dad wholeheartedly. Although he did play a lot with us children and was a good father – most of the time – I can neither forget nor forgive the beatings. For a long time I wanted to take revenge, but in the end I just felt pity for the old man.'

'And Mum? What did you think of her affair?'

'As I said, I could never be certain until the DNA test, but... ' He took a deep breath and went on in a softer voice. ' ... You know, Jonas, I felt deserted when you came into the world, and you were right that I never wanted a brother. You got her unconditional love. I got homework supervision from her and was grounded when I got bad school marks.'

'But she was so proud of your achievements, your career as a judge.'

'I felt she always wanted me to take sides – take *her* side – most of the time. They argued a lot, struggling through life with very little money. And always quarrelling over the housekeeping.'

'I do remember that!'

'I tried hard to mediate between our parents – perhaps that's why I became a judge! Oh, that reminds me. What did you think of Dad's note?'

'What do you mean?

'You know, the scribbled message he wrote before he died. I found it after you left, scanned it in and sent it over to you as an attachment, along with the hospital report.'

'I must have missed that, or accidentally deleted it. What did it say?'

'I'll send it again now. Talk about it later, if you like. And remember: I'm always here for you.'

A few minutes later, I downloaded the PDF.

To my sons

We are in your debt. There is nothing I can do now to atone for our past actions.

Helmut, did you become a judge for my sake? Have you found sufficient evidence to prosecute – have you? Have you pronounced judgment on me yet?

Jonas, did you become a history teacher so you could unravel our past? I'm sure you'll have found the film roll and ciné film. There are no more secrets in my darkroom. Would your lives have been different if you had not grown up in the shadow of our monstrous past? My father once said to us, 'You're the future of Germany.' I sincerely hope you make a better job of it than we did.

All my love,

Dad

I sat there for a long time, head buried in my hands, eyes welling up. Honest and dignified in the end. *Thank you, Dad.*

He knew we'd be struggling with our 'inheritance'. This lasting burden of our history – the political and cultural baggage we're lugging around with us. How many generations will it take to lift the burden from our shoulders? When will we stop squatting in the tepid bath of our parents' past?

Sam and I met up at the university to discuss the very last chapter of *Fractured Lives*. I couldn't help criticising him for his premature intervention, thus ruining our plans for Elsa's extradition, as well as the search for Mum's diary and, most important of all, my relationship with Bettina.

'Why on earth did you contact the Wiesenthal Centre without consulting me first? You've scuppered our whole project. I can't tell you how angry and disappointed I am.'

'I'm really sorry. I didn't think they'd react so swiftly in passing the information on to the German prosecutors. I did tell them we were still gathering evidence of her involvement in the extermination camp.'

'Did you also see the appeal for information on Nazi war criminals on their website? They were offering a 25,000 Euro reward. Is that why—?' I shouted.

'No, absolutely not. This is about complicity in murder, about justice for the survivors.'

'Well, I'm not sure if there'll be any justice in the end, due to your intervention. Elsa got a letter from the authorities and now she's disappeared.'

I walked out, slamming the door behind me. I didn't

want to go into any further detail; to tell him how Elsa had surprised us in her study, furiously waving the extradition letter. The whole conversation with Sam had left a bitter taste in my mouth. Had it damaged our friendship for good? I couldn't be sure.

On Wednesday morning, I walked past Hampstead Heath towards the Tube station. The scenery was postcard-perfect – the sky, coated with a fine white veil, softened the gleam of the sunlight. The gardens at the edge of the park were strewn with wind-blown blossoms – the shredded petals from the white wisteria resembled soft confetti left after a wedding. Lovers, arms tightly wrapped around one another, ambled through the park. The scene evoked memories of walking hand in hand with Bettina along Regent's Canal before our boat trip. Although still fresh in my memory, it all seemed such a long time ago now. I had stood once again at that point in my life when I was able to take a different direction and had another chance for an enduring relationship. Now it was fading away like a nostalgic dream.

The tube to King's Cross St Pancras didn't take long and the British Library was just round the corner. I found Bettina in her office, hidden behind a pile of newly arrived books. Her colleague, a woman in her late twenties I would guess, opened the door. She gave me a serious look through her heavy black-rimmed glasses.

'You've come about the coat,' she said sharply, not asking me to come in.

Bettina rose slowly from behind her books. She appeared even paler than usual, wearing a black polo neck over a dark, knee-length skirt. A frown gathered on her forehead as our eyes met.

'Your coat's in the cloakroom downstairs. I'll come with you,' she said, pushing past the open door. I felt her colleague's gaze upon me, as if she was checking me out. She gave me a quizzical look as I dropped a sealed envelope on Bettina's desk.

The empty cloakroom had an ultra-modern shape, like a giant pumpkin cut in two. From a large curved rail mounted on to what looked like tall silver organ pipes hung a large number of coat hangers, some empty, some clothed with light coats and jackets. Opposite this half-moon shape, facing the street, was a brick wall with an oblong window.

I spotted my raincoat straight away and took it off its hanger. Bettina stood by the window and said nothing. Pushing the thick auburn hair back a little from her ears, she turned her head sideways. I was struck by the clenched white hands, her absent lost look as she gazed outside.

How can you write silence on a page? Is there such a thing as a guilty silence? A resonating silence of pent-up feelings. I held my breath, imagining I was standing on the edge of a cliff.

Then, decisively, as if she'd finally made up her mind to have it out, she turned to face me. Her sentences flew off the line like a kayak racing over the edge of a waterfall.

'That's it, then. I don't believe you ever really loved me. You used me for one thing only: to get to the bottom of your parents' history, to discover your mum's diary, to find out about your dad. Were they committed Nazis to the bitter end, like my aunt? What satisfaction would it give you to see a frail eighty-year-old woman stand trial and go to prison for the rest of her life? What would you have done if she had been your mother? Your mother was a BdM leader and a staunch supporter of the NS regime. Does that make her any less guilty?'

'At least she didn't work in a concentration camp.' I flew off the handle. 'Why the hell do you always try to appease your aunt, never wanting to confront her with her war crimes? Why have you never asked her about the Groß-Rosen camp?'

'I didn't want to know. And I don't want to know now. I can't bear it. She was like a mother to me when my parents died. Sometimes it's better to leave the past *in* the past. Don't you agree?'

'No, I certainly don't.' I turned around and walked a few steps away from her.

'I feel so cheap, Jonas. Was I just a convenient research tool for you, with a bit of sex thrown in for good measure? You spend most of your time teaching and researching, but what about real life and happiness? Why are you just stuck in the past all the time, researching your family's history? You know, it's difficult to comprehend that the person I thought I knew, and knew intimately, could be so cruel. We could have had a future together. Did you really love me, Jonas?' Her voice sounded plaintive. She tugged at my arm and made me face her.

'I am *so* very sorry, Bettina. Believe me, I didn't mean to use you like that. I do love you, with all my heart.'

Her stern face softened a fraction, but the frown between her brows remained visible. Those big brown eyes of hers, that mouth with its delicately lifted upper lip – both had a resentful sadness about them. A powerful blend of desolation and outrage, longing mixed with fury. When she'd hesitated for a moment to let me into Elsa's room, did she feel a cold premonition of a different kind of betrayal? This time, not the humiliation of being left for a younger woman, but being used for ulterior motives by an older man. Did she really *mean* it when she declared that she never wanted to see me again? Had I humiliated her beyond repair?

'Is there nothing I can do to win you back?' I asked, resting my hands softly on her shoulders. Bettina wrinkled her nose contemptuously.

'The worst of it is,' she said calmly, after a pause, 'you're right to want to know about your family's past. I understand why you wanted so much to find out the truth – not just about my aunt, but first and foremost about your parents – even if the outcome was a guilty verdict. From a very young age I grew up without parents, so I never really experienced their love. But you did, and now you seem to have lost that feeling, haven't you? And *our* relationship? I wish I'd never fallen in love with you. It has all been a fraud, a trick to get me to like you, under false pretences.'

'No, it hasn't,' I protested. 'My love for you is real and hasn't changed.'

She sat down on the single chair in the room, folded her hands, concealing them between her legs, her long hair falling over her bent head. Then, quite suddenly, she stood up, raised her hands and punched me in the chest with her fists, over and over. A broken-hearted woman who so wanted to turn back the wheel of time. It was a drumbeat of muted blows, an eruption of helpless fury, an assault against the loss of happy times.

The blows grew weaker and slower, the emotions subsided. I tried in vain to pull her towards me. Exhausted, Bettina walked backwards into the room, sat back down on the chair and started to weep. Alarmed and apprehensive, I wondered what I should say next. I'd been shaken by seeing Bettina burst into tears, and wanted to make a conscious effort to soften the blow.

'Perhaps I'm just not very good at relationships … I understand that you're very upset about everything that's happened, but it'll all come right,' I tried to soothe her. 'We can always—'

'I can't see how I can ever trust you again. You can't base a relationship on a lie. I think we're past repair.' She wiped away her tears, straightened up and got herself under control again.

'By the way, I took a copy of your mother's original diary – librarians are always told to make backups of valuable items. But you'll never see a single page, never find out the truth.'

'But how can you not—?'

My sentence did not need completing. On that note, she left without a backward glance.

'I never meant to hurt you.'

My words echoed through the open door like an aching hollowness. I sat down on the chair, slumped, head cupped in my hands, eyes closed. The chair still felt warm. Was this the way things had to be? A strong hatred to destroy a love, to erect a wall to protect herself? Was this how our story ended – another tale of fractured lives? Bettina had become part of the texture of my own personal history.

Family research lures you into a web which cannot be disentangled without touching, and sometimes breaking, other threads.

Sitting on a platform high above the nave in the heart of All Saints Cathedral in Camden Town, the members of the choir are murmuring in muted voices. They're elegantly dressed in black – the men in cream ties, the women wearing cream anemones in their buttonholes. The audience have taken their seats and a few latecomers are hurrying in. The seat beside me is still empty. The first item on the programme is Hubert Parry's *Songs of Farewell*. Will Bettina have picked up the concert ticket I left on her desk at work? The doors are about to close …

Printed in Poland
by Amazon Fulfillment
Poland Sp. z o.o., Wrocław

49510280R00150